Locked Within

Locked Within

Paul Anthony Shortt

To [illegible],

Thanks [illegible]

[illegible]

8/11/12

WiDo Publishing • Salt Lake City

WiDo Publishing
Salt Lake City, Utah
widopublishing.com

This book is a work of fiction. Names, characters, places, organizations and incidents are either products of the author's imagination or are used fictitiously. Any resemblance to actual persons, living or dead, events or organizations is entirely coincidental.

Cover design by Steven Novak
Book design by Marny K. Parkin

Print ISBN: 978-1-937178-25-3

Printed in the United States of America

For my son,
Conor William Henry Shortt

Chapter One

EACH MOVE FLOWED PERFECTLY INTO THE NEXT; one unending motion. Nathan Shepherd whipped his rattan sticks into position with practiced accuracy. The precise technique for each strike and counter flowed from his memory, shifting his stance so that it seemed as though no move could have been made without the one that came before it.

His muscles burned, alive with adrenaline. Nathan pushed on, reaching the edge of his strength for just a moment before hitting his second wind. Renewed energy coursed through his limbs with every beat of his heart. Nathan began kicking in broad sweeps as he worked through his routine. He wasn't just an office clerk working out in a downtown dojo. He was a warrior. A soldier on a battlefield. A champion in single combat.

Nathan brought his foot down at a poor angle and twisted it, falling to the floor. He landed on his tailbone and felt pain shoot up his spine. He winced and sat back up. His vision blurred briefly and his head spun as the ache in his muscles returned even stronger than before.

"Too far, too soon," a voice said from the doorway.

Nathan stood slowly and recovered his stance before bowing to Hector Morita, the owner of the dojo. Though he was a portly man in glasses, Nathan had seen him in sparring matches against up to three opponents at once, winning. Hector returned the bow but waved to the clock on the wall. "I've got to get ready for my morning class, and I think you need to get to work."

"I've been late before," Nathan said.

"That's not balance, and you know it."

Nathan smiled and picked up his rattan sticks. "Can I use the shower before I go?"

"Of course."

"How did I look, anyway?"

"Your speed's improving, and you pick up new technique better than most of my advanced students."

"But?"

Hector pressed his hand against Nathan's chest. "This." He tapped his fingers against Nathan's forehead. "And this. You use one or the other, never both. Until you can balance your head and your heart, you're going to keep falling on your ass."

Nathan laughed. "I'll remember that." He bowed again to Hector before heading to the showers to wash off the sweat and change into his work clothes. Just black slacks and a light grey shirt. He packed his rattan sticks and gym clothes into a duffel bag.

He'd left his car at a parking meter. Having better choice of parking spots was one of the advantages of never sleeping properly. His mind drifted to the dreams. The nightmares. Blood on snow. A sword in his hand. Pain in his stomach. Nathan pushed the thought away even as the images filled his mind's eye. He got into his car and drove to work.

The familiar smells of Manhattan drifted through the air conditioning as Nathan drove through the streets. Heavy exhaust fumes mixed with the sticky aroma of fried hot nuts from street vendors and the added intrusion of scents from early morning coffee shops. It was a heady mix that stuck to Nathan's senses like glue. And he loved it.

Rounding a corner onto Chambers Street, Nathan made his way to the City Hall parking lot, waving to the security guard as he drove in. He retrieved his duffel bag from the back seat before locking his car and headed across the street to the Hall of Records.

The ten-story building loomed over the street in all its ancient glory. Nathan took a glance up at the statues of past city mayors and figureheads amid the front colonnade, high above the entrance. Most places in the city made him feel cramped and suffocated. Some, like this one, were different. He ran his fingertips across the wall as he stepped inside, breathing in deeply. The stone felt alive. It was strong and unyielding. The air was filled with a sense of purpose and history. Nathan walked past the other arrivals, through the grand lobby bathed in warm light from above. He took his time, enjoying the echo of his shoes on the marble floor.

Nathan's desk was tucked into a corner with a wall behind him and a window looking out toward City Hall.

He glanced at the photograph of his girlfriend, Laura, sitting on his desk. She hadn't smiled like that in a while. Nathan turned to his computer and started writing an e-mail.

Cynthia

Are we still on for tonight?

Nathan

It was a couple of hours later when the reply came in.

Yes. I've got something for you I think you'll like. Just be careful, I don't want to get caught. We're taking enough risks as it is.

Cynthia

After that, Nathan carried on through the rest of his day with unthinking repetition. There were so many more important things on his mind than filing certificates and processing documentation requests. Unfortunately, getting into the office late and waiting for Cynthia's e-mail had left him behind, and it was dark by the time he left work and pulled out of the parking lot.

Reflected light flowed over Nathan's car as he drove along the city streets. He cursed the ever-growing pile of paperwork he'd left on his desk and tried to avoid looking at the digital clock on his dashboard. His cell phone beeped an electronic tone over and over from his pocket. Nathan fished it out and answered.

"I was beginning to think you'd given up on this. Where are you?"

Cynthia. It sounded like she was outdoors.

Nathan turned a corner. "Just coming up to you now."

"Good," Cynthia said. "One of your cases is nearby."

Nathan took the next right. A green SUV cut him off as he rounded a corner and Nathan blared his horn. "Damn son of a—"

A dark-skinned man shot a look through the passenger window as the SUV drove on.

A second later, Nathan found Cynthia standing next to her car, wearing a red mac and a green scarf. Nathan parked and got out, throwing on his jacket more for the extra pocket space than for warmth. He tucked his keys into one pocket and a bottle of water into the other.

"Ready?" he asked.

Cynthia nodded. "Right with you. Just, let's be careful, okay? This doesn't feel like the last time."

"Exactly. This time I'm getting involved."

"Do you really think there's something to this?" Cynthia tugged at her coat. "That it's more than just coincidence?"

Nathan no longer believed in coincidence. His girlfriend Laura had once referred to his habits as apophenia. He worried that she might be right. But then, something about a case would call to him. Like this one.

"Look, Cynthia you don't have to do this. Really, I'll be fine on my own."

She shook her head. "No, I'm in. But if it gets dangerous, promise me we leave and call the police? You haven't seen the forensics on this. It's freaky."

There was no time to dwell on fears. Nathan took the sports bag from his car and slung it over his shoulder.

"What's all that?" Cynthia asked.

"Just some things I might need," he answered. "Flashlight, first aid kit, map of the city, a hammer, some duct tape, that sort of thing."

Cynthia frowned. "A hammer? First aid kit? I'm not sure I like the sound of this."

He grinned and gave a shrug. "Hey, you wanted to come along. Now where are we going?"

Cynthia pointed across the street to a Laundromat. "The parking lot there."

Nathan nodded and hurried across the street. Cynthia jogged to keep up with him. "What's the date on this one?" he asked her.

"September 4th, 1993."

Nathan scribbled notes on a small pad and tucked it into the inside pocket of his jacket. He stepped over to a service door for the Laundromat and took a digital camera from his sports bag.

"This is where the body was found, right?" He knelt down for a better shot of the concrete step at the foot of the door. The glow from the street lights didn't provide much light to work by, but Nathan managed to get a couple of decent shots.

"Yes." Cynthia stepped back a little. "How did you know?"

Nathan looked back over his shoulder. It wasn't as though the doorway was highly visible from the street. It would have been a good place to jump someone, or leave a body. As good as a public parking lot in the middle of Manhattan can be, anyway. "Just a hunch, I suppose."

Nathan looked around the parking lot, noting small details like the license plates of the three cars parked there, the spot where someone had dumped the remains of a burger on the ground, an area on the wall of the launderette where once three bullets had struck it, leaving small holes now worn wide with age.

At one end of the parking lot was the entrance to a back alley. There was little light, except for what came from the far end where the alley opened back out onto a street. Something was moving in the light breeze, silhouetted against the distant street lights. It was long and yellow, like a strip of tape stuck to a wall. He walked to the alley.

"Where are you going now?" Cynthia hurried after him.

"Another hunch," he told her.

He was right. It was police tape. It had been stuck across a doorway in four long diagonal strips, one of which had come loose and was wafting around in the breeze from a subway grille. A broken light hung over the doorway.

"What's this building?" he asked. "Do you know?"

Cynthia looked out at the street. "It used to be a youth hostel. It's due to be renovated and turned into apartments. Look, we really shouldn't be here."

Nathan watched how her eyes darted away from him. "Did something happen here?"

Cynthia nodded.

"When?" The excitement rose in his voice. "Recently?"

"It was about a week ago," she said. "A woman's body was found inside. Why?"

Nathan pulled out his notebook and flashlight so quickly that he nearly dropped his camera. He shone the light on the pages.

"Look, here," he said in quick breaths. "The cases I asked about, the ones I wanted from you, the deaths happened in ten-year intervals, all within a couple of months." He pointed down the alleyway, back to the parking lot. "Back there, 1993. Right here," he pointed to the taped-over door, "a stone's throw away, we have another one, twenty years later."

"Your point?" Cynthia stared back at him blankly.

He shook his head, frustrated. "Tell me how they died. The people on my list."

"Cardiac failure," she said.

"And the woman found in this building?"

"Also cardiac failure."

Nathan gestured at the building with his flashlight. "You see? All deaths due to cardiac failure, happening in ten-year intervals. I'll bet the other deaths happened near here, too."

He swept the beam of his flashlight around the area, half to emphasize his point, and half to get a quick look at surrounding buildings for later reference.

"They did," Cynthia admitted. "But Nathan, cardiac failure doesn't mean anything. Their hearts stopped. It's a classification given any time the coroner can't provide a more clear cause of death. It's like saying natural causes."

Nathan shone his light on the lock of the door handle. "Maybe it's time someone found a more clear cause of death."

The door had an old mortise lock. The frame was chipped and cracked and looked in need of replacement. Nathan took a step back and kicked the door, just to the left of the lock. The door shook and he heard wood begin to splinter.

"Jesus, Nathan!" Cynthia cried. "What the hell?"

"Do you know how to pick a lock?"

Cynthia shook her head. Nathan kicked the door again, ignoring her protests, breaking off a piece of the doorframe. With one more solid kick, the latch tore from the frame and the door swung open. He aimed his flashlight into the building and stepped inside. Shadows flitted around, cast by his light. He was in a rear hallway which stank of damp and animal feces. Soggy, moldy wallpaper hung in tattered clumps from the walls, and a rat scurried away as he ventured deeper inside.

Nathan looked back to the doorway. "You coming?"

There were no sounds of shouting or sirens. Either no one had heard them break in, or no one cared.

"I'll, uh … keep a lookout," Cynthia called back.

Nathan ventured through the doorway, checking rooms as he passed. Most of the walls were coated in cracked paint, exposing the drywall underneath. Bare cables reached out from exposed power outlets and light fittings. Lumps of old plaster crunched underfoot.

Nathan came to a corner where he saw the faded remains of a chalk outline showing where the victim had been sprawled on the floor. He took a few pictures of the scene.

He didn't notice any old bloodstains, but there were markings on the wallpaper that looked relatively fresh. Upon closer examination, he saw that they were slashes, like someone had taken a sharp knife and scored the walls, cutting down into the drywall underneath. He shone the light around the hallway, picking out several more marks, seeing the patterns where someone had disturbed the filth and muck on the floor with their feet.

Nathan guessed that two people had been fighting here. The slashes on the walls were at the right level for combatants swinging blades at roughly chest or head height. He peeled back the torn paper on some of the slashes, and figured that they could likely have been caused by two people standing opposite one another.

No. Only one was armed. While some of the marks were long and straight lines striking alone across the wall, there were other, more numerous ones, grouped together in sets of three or four, shorter, and sometimes curved. *Claws.*

Nathan paused for a moment and mentally chided himself for jumping to crazy conclusions. *Murder. This was a murder. Had to be.* He called down the corridor to Cynthia. "Where there any weapons found at the scene at the Laundromat? Any large cuts on the body?"

"No," she shouted back, leaning into the doorway a little to take a look.

"So someone fought back," he said. The killer wasn't the one with the sword. Nathan guided the flashlight over the cuts and down to the floor where he saw patches of dried blood.

A noise disturbed his train of thought. Creaking floorboards overhead. "Stay outside," he shouted to Cynthia, as he ran upstairs to the source of the sound.

Nathan came up onto a bare landing and was slammed against the wall by someone moving from the shadows. His attacker wore dark clothing, his face stark and pale. He drew back a fist as if to strike. With only a split second to act, Nathan brought the end of the flashlight down on his face. He'd heard somewhere that nightclub bouncers and security staff at big concerts used heavy duty flashlights because they can be used as an efficient club without breaking.

Someone else ran toward them. It was a slender man, with a short blonde ponytail and a narrow face. He had the look of a predatory rodent. "Son of a bitch!" he exclaimed and pulled the fallen man back by the arm.

Nathan backed off, holding up both hands. The blonde man grabbed him in a choke hold, knocking the flashlight away with his free hand. It fell to the ground and rolled to cast an eerie half-light around the landing.

"Stay out of our way." His frenzied eyes flared with yellow and red. Long fangs grew in his jaw right before Nathan's eyes. "Whoever you and your friends are, this isn't your town." He squeezed harder around Nathan's throat.

Nathan felt his head spin as his vision faded. He made heaving, retching sounds, his lungs trying to draw air through the crushing grip. He heard the sound of more footsteps running on creaky wood as his legs gave way.

His two attackers ran past him, leaving Nathan to slump onto the floor. Glass shattered down the hall. Several people came running from upstairs. The first, a dark-skinned man, dropped to kneel next to Nathan, a shotgun in his hands. It was the man from the green SUV.

"Are you all right? Did you get bit?" he asked.

"Huh?" Nathan's mind drifted back to the blonde man's face. Pale and savage, a pair of long fangs growing even as he spoke.

"No time to sterilize," the black man muttered. He lifted Nathan to his feet and pulled his head from side to side, then lifted his arms and pulled back his sleeves. "All right, looks like you're clean." He craned his neck to look down the hall. "Cadence, do you see them?"

"The creature's gone, Adams. It dropped its victim on the street." A woman's voice. "The vampires have cleared out. We need to get out of here."

"I'm okay," Nathan rasped. "Tell me what's going on."

"Sorry, kid. Do yourself a favor and forget this. Your girlfriend outside hasn't seen us, we got in from the roof of the next building, and that's how we're leaving. You go back downstairs and get out of here."

"But—"

"Go! Now!" He ran to the stairs, followed quickly by his two companions. Nathan took his flashlight and staggered down the stairs, almost falling out into the alley.

"My God," Cynthia said, helping him up. "You look like hell. Are you okay?"

"I'm okay, don't worry."

"You're bleeding! What happened in there?"

Nathan wiped his lip. "Oh, uh, I walked into a door. Look, we have to get moving."

She frowned. "Why?"

"We just do," he said. "I saw … something. Come on."

They hurried back to the car, where Cynthia dug out her first aid kit. Nathan explained what had just happened while she worked.

"You can't be serious." Cynthia dabbed antiseptic on Nathan's lip. "So you got attacked by two vampires, and three vampire hunters came running after them and saved you?"

"Look, I'm not saying I saw Sarah Michelle Gellar carrying wooden stakes or anything, but I did see that guy grow fangs from nowhere. And the other group seemed to have some idea of what was going on." He looked around, hearing sirens in the distance. "We should go. Laura and I are having dinner with my dad. Can you do me a favor?"

"Nathan, I'm having second thoughts about all this. Looking up forensic reports for you is one thing, but I can't be found out bringing you to crime scenes."

"Please, Cynthia? You're the only one I can turn to for this stuff."

She packed away her first aid kit and tossed it into her car. "I liked it better when this was just a hobby. But if you think there's something serious going on, I'll help you."

"Okay, I need you to keep an eye out at work. There should be a fresh body coming in from here. I need any information you can get on it."

Cynthia nodded, sliding into her car. "I'm going to lose my job, I just know it."

Chapter Two

"Anything yet?" Adams leaned back against the wall. He was sitting on the bed of their small hostel room.

Cadence would have preferred something with more privacy, but they'd had to come to New York on short notice. She sat in a lotus position on her bed, having changed into a t-shirt and sweatpants after showering. Spread out before her was a large map of Manhattan. She held a quartz pendant on a silver chain in her right hand, moving it over the map. Her left hand was palm up and at a right angle to her torso. As she moved her hand, the pendant swung in circles. The spell was simple but required concentration and time. Interruptions weren't helping.

"Not yet." Cadence focused on the lock of hair, tied together with a piece of string, lying in the palm of her left hand. As she drew energy into her body, it passed through the hair, giving her a connection to its owner. "This isn't as easy as it looks, you know."

Suddenly the pendant twitched and she felt a pull. Cadence let the force guide her and she noted the trail it drew in the air. When it was done, she grabbed a permanent marker and drew a line along it.

"Got it," she said, falling back on a pillow. She took the glass of water on the bed stand and drained it. "Now can we eat?"

Adams nodded. "Lane won't be much longer. Then we can eat and get some rest. I want us on the trail early."

Cadence rubbed the ache out of her arms. "What about that guy tonight, what if he knows about the creature? What if he finds it? Whoever he is, he doesn't seem up to something like this. Not after what we saw tonight."

"I don't know," Adams admitted.

"You felt it," Cadence said. "Didn't you? He's green, sure, but it's there, untapped. He's one of us."

"There aren't supposed to be any of us active in this city, not since the war. This could cause problems. Big ones."

"Tell me again why I keep working for you?"

Adams grinned. "Because I pay you well."

Cadence brushed her damp hair. "Well, next time you can halve my pay and get me my own room."

Nathan ran through questions in his head as he drove up Bowery. Why had Murdoch and Sullivan, one of the biggest real estate companies on the East Coast, requested that his office provide copies of the death certificates of more than a hundred people who had died between 1843 and 2003? Why had there been others at the same place earlier that night? Had he really seen men with fangs, actual fangs? He managed to calm himself before pulling up outside a gray apartment building in north Manhattan. It had a mess of blue and green spray paint across the front doors.

There was a set of doorbells half-fixed to the doorframe. Nathan pressed one and waited for the response. "Hello?" came a crackly voice.

"Hey, Dad, it's me."

A buzzer sounded and Nathan headed inside toward the stairs. The place had a functioning elevator, but Nathan liked the exercise, and only needed to go up two floors. His father lived in an apartment at the end of a long hallway. The building was in disrepair, but that came more from general neglect than vandalism. The neighborhood had grown rougher over the years, but the gangs left Mike Shepherd and his neighbors alone.

About eleven years ago, Mike had pulled four local kids from a burning building, going back inside twice to make sure he'd found everyone he could. No heroic act went unpunished, however, and the fire had left its mark. Nathan's dad spent months in the hospital being treated for burns to his arms and back. Nerve damage had forced him into early retirement. His wife, Nathan's mother, passed away a few years later, so Mike moved into this small apartment. It was affordable and easy for him to manage.

Mike had been a tall, broad-shouldered man before he'd been hurt, the strongest person Nathan knew. He was a man who carried children to safety, ignoring the flames scorching his skin.

The door opened and Nathan was greeted by a slightly hunched, gray-haired old man, smiling up at him. Both men shared the same squint and thin lips but they had some differences. Mike's nose was broader, and crooked from an old break. Nathan's face was more sharp, his jaw tight. At least he knew he'd keep his hair when he got old and lose the russet coloring instead. They hugged and Mike kissed his son on the cheek.

"You're late," he said. "Laura's already here."

"Yeah, sorry about that." Nathan stepped into the small apartment. "I was a little late getting out of work. I've got my cell phone with me, though." He took off his coat and hung it up on a stand next to his dad's old duffel coat.

Mike gave a short laugh as he circled the small brown couch in the living room and headed to the kitchen. "You never answer that thing. Come on, food's ready. My specialty."

Nathan glanced at the shelves along one wall near the front door. Photos of him and his parents sat neatly between collections of books ranging from the latest mystery novels to encyclopedias and books on chemistry and history. A simple wooden frame hung on the far wall, near the television and Mike's battered leather recliner. Inside was a medal pinned to some green felt backing. Although Nathan couldn't make out the writing on the small plaque beneath the medal, he knew what the words said.

For Bravery in the Line of Duty
Presented To
Michael Shepherd
Hook & Ladder Co. 8 New York City Fire Department

"You were supposed to meet me at the hospital after my shift," Laura, still wearing her doctor's scrubs, leaned against the kitchen counter holding a glass of water. She frowned, pursing her lips, and tucked a short, straight strand back under her hair band. "You have a cut on your lip."

"Oh, that. Yeah, I walked into a door at work."

Laura sat down at the pine table dotted with coffee-ring stains. "You should've called if you were going to be late."

"I'm really sorry," Nathan said. "Did you have to get a cab?"

She shook her head. "No, I got a ride from a friend."

Nathan and his dad sat down at the table. Mike's specialty was a large order from the local Chinese takeout. Nathan helped himself to a spring roll while his dad set down a beer each. He handed one to Laura, but she shook her head.

"It was great you could get tonight off, Laura." Mike grabbed a carton of noodles and stabbed his chopsticks in. She had been working mostly night shifts for over a month.

Laura nodded, spooning out some food onto a plate while the men ate straight from the boxes. She ate with a knife and fork, ignoring Mike's offer of chopsticks.

"How're you two doing?" Mike asked.

"Fine," they both said together. Laura stared at Nathan across the table. He looked back down to his food.

"Excuse me," Laura said. She stood and went into the bathroom.

Mike leaned over and spoke softly. "You ought to do the right thing, you know. Ask the girl to marry you."

Nathan had never felt particularly religious, but he'd been raised Catholic—his grandmother had come to New York from Ireland—and his dad still kept a set of rosary beads in his bedside locker. Marriage and family were a big deal. They were things he had wanted for years, despite his lapsed faith.

"I know," Nathan said. "But I don't want it to be something I do just to try and fix things, you know? If … well, *when* I ask her, it shouldn't be some quick fix to our problems."

Mike swallowed back the last of his beer. "Son, you're a lot smarter than you look." He got up to get himself another drink. "You got your mother's brains."

"What'd I get from you?"

Mike sat back down. "Your looks. You ask me, we both got short-changed there."

After dinner, Mike took Nathan aside. "Listen, son, are you free tomorrow night?"

"Yeah."

"I've got something I want to show you."

"What is it?"

He shook his head. "You'll have to wait and see. Tomorrow night, I'll call you, okay?"

"Sure thing. 'Night, Dad."

After leaving the apartment, Nathan and Laura walked in silence to the car. She sat in the passenger seat with her arms folded, gazing away from him. It was a long and tense drive back to Queens.

At home Nathan said, "You could've at least tried to make conversation." He tossed his coat onto an armchair, but Laura swooped in and scooped it up, placing it on the coat stand next to the door.

"I'm tired from work," Laura said, heading to the kitchen. Nathan went in after her. "And you don't have to keep following me."

"Jeez, I was just going to get a drink." He went to the fridge and pulled out a bottle of white wine. "What's this about?" He opened the wine and poured out a glass before placing it back and shutting the fridge door.

She fixed him with a stare and pulled the door open again, taking out some juice. "You were late because you were with Cynthia, weren't you?"

"Who told you that?"

"I called the Medical Examiner's Office." She poured a glass and placed the juice back in the fridge, shutting the door forcefully. "I wanted to meet her for lunch tomorrow. Her boss said she'd already left. To meet you."

Nathan nodded. "Right."

"Why wouldn't you tell me you were meeting her?"

"It was just coffee after work," he said, hoping he could lie well enough. "I didn't think it would matter."

"You should have told me."

"Told you? What do you think we got up to? I meet her for coffee all the time."

"Exactly!"

"Are you really going there? She's one of your oldest friends. I've known the two of you since you were in med school together. Neither of us would ever do anything to hurt you."

"That's not what I mean, Nathan." She swallowed back a large gulp of juice. "Why Cynthia? For all these years, why is she the one? You go for coffee, you have lunch, and you talk. Why not me? When was the last time you came to me when you were worried about work? Or met me for lunch when I was working a weekend shift?"

"I tried," he said. "But you're always busy, working late. Tonight's the first night off you've had in a month."

"And instead of being on time to pick me up, you did what you always do. You went and saw Cynthia." She set the glass down. "I love Cynthia. She's been with me through so much, and I accept that you stayed friends after you two broke up in college. But," she breathed back a sob. "I need some of you too. I miss that. We used to talk for hours. All night, even. I feel like I hardly know you sometimes, now."

"I'm sorry," Nathan tried to keep speaking, but his throat felt numb. Laura rolled back her sleeves and rinsed her glass under the faucet, then walked back into the darkness of the living room and sat on the couch. He saw faint bruises on her arms. They were fresh, near her wrists. "You're hurt. What happened?"

She turned away from him. "Just leave me alone."

He stood silently for a moment, noting the shape of the bruising. They were long, encircling the forearm, like she'd been grabbed. *A violent patient?* All kinds of thugs ended up in the emergency room late at night. It wouldn't have been the first time Laura had come home with cuts or bruises from work. After a moment, he turned and left, trying to ignore the sound of her crying as he went upstairs.

Nathan considered the small, velvet-covered box he kept in the glove compartment of his car. *Not tonight, then.* During a long, hot shower his thoughts drifted away from

Laura. He could not have seen real vampires earlier that evening. It could have been a trick of the light. *Maybe they wore fake fangs?* He could have stumbled into some sick cult, one that might be involved with the deaths he was investigating.

Nathan toweled himself off and went into the bedroom, catching a glimpse of his tired, dark-blue eyes and ashen face. He wasn't a well-built man, but he wasn't skinny or overweight, either. He'd kept fit, but it showed more in his overall health than his figure. Sometimes he wondered how he'd managed to get and hang on to a woman like Laura. Tying a larger towel around his waist, he dried his hair with a smaller one. He finished, tossing the towel onto the bed, and looked in the mirror. Laura was standing behind him, her eyes red from tears.

Nathan turned as she approached. His heart beat faster. Laura's hands reached for his shoulders and pulled him close to her. She pressed her lips to his and parted them with her tongue, moving her fingers through his hair. He held her around the waist as she pulled off her scrubs and gently, but firmly, urged him to the bed.

They made love in silence. Every so often Laura would glance down at Nathan and she would shut her eyes, holding his arms down when he tried to reach up and touch her.

Afterwards Laura lay curled up in bed, facing away from Nathan. "I'm sorry," she whispered. He heard her sobbing, but she pulled away when he reached for her.

Chapter Three

NATHAN FOUND HIMSELF IN A DARK CORRIDOR, holding an old-fashioned oil lantern in one hand and a flintlock pistol in the other. Water dripped from the ceiling and outside he could hear rain pounding down. He had a thick beard, and he was limping. A shape moved from the shadows, but Nathan didn't waste his shot on an impulsive reaction. He gave chase, a long coat trailing behind him.

His quarry spun and fired a pistol. Nathan twisted and the shot missed. "Damn you, Silver!" The man sneered, flashing long teeth. Fangs. A name entered Nathan's mind. *Eli.* He was familiar. The vampire who had choked him that night. It was him. But his hair was longer, tied with a looped leather thong. He wore a loose shirt, with a sword hanging from a baldric around his shoulders.

Nathan fired as Eli charged, drawing his sword. The shot struck Eli in the chest, but he had fired too late. The sword pierced his ribs and he felt a choking sensation, like he was trying to breathe through water. Both men fell and darkness came.

In the morning, Nathan called his boss at the Department of Records to tell him he was sick and wouldn't make it in.

All his life, he had experienced dreams of other times and places. In some he was a nobleman, enjoying fine foods and clothes, in others he was poor and humble, eking out his existence as best he could. There was always violence. His dreams took him to open battle and darkened alleyway brawls. Desperate fights against people and things that would defy normal sense but were at home in the realm of his dreams.

Of them all, one of the most common was of a brutal duel where he wore heavy Roman armor, battling someone of higher rank—his superior, while women and children watched, huddled on the snow. The dream would always end with his opponent driving his sword into Nathan's stomach, then leaving him to die in the cold while the people looked on.

Trying to shake off the dream, Nathan had coffee, then he drove into Manhattan and left his car in a public parking lot. He spent the next while just walking around the streets, casting sidelong glances at every passerby. His neck still throbbed with a dull ache. Bruising had started to show where he'd been choked. Vivid images of inhuman eyes and long fangs haunted his thoughts.

Vampires or not, these people were involved in something strange. People were dying.

Someone has to do something about it.

Those other people, the ones who had saved Nathan, knew what they were doing.

"This isn't your town," Eli had said. He must have thought Nathan was one of them. Whoever they were, they weren't from New York. Nathan thought back to their car. The green SUV appeared in his mind, speeding in front of his sedan. He froze the image of the SUV from behind, building the image in his mind. New York license plates. A rental company sticker. Someone had tried to peel it away, but there was enough left to get part of the name.

Nathan hurried to a phone booth and leafed through the Yellow Pages. Speed-reading the ads for car rental companies, he was able to match up what bits of the company name he had with one in the phone book. He dialed the number on his cell phone.

"Hi," he said when he got through. "I think I hit one of your cars last night. I have the license number here and I'll pay for the damage when it's brought back in, but I'd really like to apologize to the driver myself. If I give you my cell number can you have the person who rented the car call me?"

The receptionist agreed and took Nathan's number. He kept walking, reaching the docks before someone called.

"Hello?"

"Who is this?" A rough, baritone voice. Nathan recognized it from the night before. It belonged to the one called Adams.

"Mr. Adams, my name is Nathan Shepherd. You saved my life last night."

"I don't think we have anything to say to each other, Mr. Shepherd." A hint of an accent. Boston?

"That's where you're wrong," he said. "Something's happening in this city. People are being hurt, and I figure you're trying to do something about it. I want in."

"No," Adams said. "You don't. The way you handled yourself last night shows you don't know enough to take care of yourself. You're more likely to get hurt than to make a difference." He paused while Nathan said nothing.

"I'm not trying to insult you," Adams went on. "I've been doing this for a long time. Listen. If you really want to help, tell me everything you know."

"Not much," Nathan said. "But I know things. I have dreams about being someone else in another place and time. I'm involved. I'm as much a part of this as you are."

"You don't have a clue. Look, just stay away from all of this, okay? You're not ready."

"Well then, I'll keep investigating this myself. I may get hurt, even killed. You sure you can live with that?"

"Yeah," he replied. "Pretty sure I can. You want to get yourself killed, Shepherd, go ahead. But I can't afford to babysit you. You're on the doorstep of a dangerous world, and I won't risk my people to protect someone who can't take a hint." He hung up.

Nathan leaned against a railing, looking out across the bay. If Adams wouldn't tell him what was going on, he'd have to figure it out on his own.

Chapter Four

NATHAN SPENT AN UNPRODUCTIVE TWO HOURS AT an Internet café searching websites dedicated to myth and folklore; or about people who wore molded fangs and drank blood as part of bizarre sex acts, but nothing of any real use. He needed reliable facts to go up against these people and find out what they had to do with Murdoch and Sullivan requesting over a hundred years' worth of death certificates from his department.

Finally, as he was about ready to give up, Cynthia called.

"Tell me you've got something," he said, handing over money to pay for his coffee and Internet usage.

"I don't know exactly what I've got, but God I can't believe I'm saying this." Nathan heard her take a breath. "I think you might be on to something."

He blinked. "Come again?"

"I don't want to talk about it over the phone. Meet me in Battery Park?"

"Sure, see you there." Nathan left the café and headed straight to the park.

Cynthia was already sitting on a bench facing out over the harbor when he arrived. She looked pale, even for someone who spent daylight hours under fluorescent lights cutting open dead bodies.

He sat beside her. "You okay?"

She handed him a folder. Inside were medical reports and photographs. He recognized them as being pictures of the building from the night before. There were photographs of a bearded man whose face was twisted into a grotesque visage of horror. The eyes had rolled back, the cornea showing from behind the eyelid. His mouth was wide open, his skin gaunt, stretched and pulled almost cartoonishly. His tongue lay over his bottom lip, all shrunken and dark. Nathan recoiled at the image.

"We're still waiting on an ID," Cynthia said. "He was found on the street outside the building last night. Rigor mortis hadn't set in, so whatever did this to him, did it not long before we got there."

Nathan kept leafing through the pages until he came to a picture of a Hispanic man with the same tormented expression. A sudden jolt of revulsion and intuition hit him.

"This is the person they found at the Laundromat twenty years ago," Cynthia said. "Name on his ID was Pedro Flores. He's a real mystery. No injuries, nothing back on the toxicology tests, and he was in fairly good health. His heart just stopped beating."

"But he suffered. I mean, look at him. Something did that to him. And why are you giving me this now? You said you weren't going to hand over the reports."

"You said yourself this one was different from the kinds of cases we used to follow in the news." Cynthia tugged at the end of her sleeve. "Here." She handed Nathan another folder.

The first file inside included a photograph of a middle-aged woman. Her mouth was stretched open like Pedro Flores's. The next was the same, this time a younger man, maybe just out of his teens. The files went on, the photographs becoming older and more faded.

"Are these what I think they are?" Nathan found his hands shaking.

"These are the people whose case numbers you gave me. The woman's name is Miranda Grange. She was the one found in that building you went into last night. A caller from a neighboring building reported seeing someone lying on the roof. Police found her fully clothed, some minor lacerations to her arms, but no sign of serious trauma. Just her face twisted like she was terrified or in horrible pain. When I saw that Flores's face had the same expression, I pulled the others. They're all like that, Nathan. Even the ones going back too far to have photographs have matching descriptions of the bodies."

"A hundred and sixty years of people being killed in the same way," he said. Vampires were starting to sound less crazy. "We're going to find out who, or what, is doing this. And we're going to stop it."

"How?" she asked. "I'm not going to pretend to understand how these deaths are connected, but getting involved is a bad idea. We should send a tip off to the police like we usually do." She reached across and held his hand. "I don't think Laura would want either of us getting hurt, do you?"

"I'm not going to let anyone hurt you," Nathan said, as though that would be a comfort. He was, after all, just some guy who worked in an office. He punched in at nine and went home at five. What did he know about killing monsters? "This woman. Miranda Grange." He leafed through the documents. "She's the first victim since the last batch of murders ten years ago. We'll start with her. What do we know?"

"Well," Cynthia said, leaning across him to turn the pages. "She was found with a sword, about three feet long, straight blade. She was wearing a Kevlar vest and carrying a 9 millimeter semi-automatic. Ballistics came up with no matches for any reported crimes, but the paperwork was sloppy and rushed, like someone wanted this put away quickly. Police contacted her next of kin in Boston. No family, just some friends. They were about to send the body home for burial. But I think this latest death might cause some delays there."

He looked up. "Boston? Miranda Grange is from Boston?"

Cynthia nodded. "Why?"

"Who did the police contact as her next of kin?"

She thought for a moment. "Andrews? Adams? Something like that."

"Adams and his two partners," he said. "The people from last night, they're from Boston, I'm sure of it."

"What?"

"I spoke to Adams on the phone. Found them through a rental company sticker on their car." He rubbed the light stubble along his jaw. "They're not here for the vampires. They're here for Miranda Grange. They're here to find out who killed her."

"That's a bit of a leap, isn't it?"

Nathan shook his head and began jabbing at the files with his finger. "No, look here. It says Miranda Grange was dead for approximately three days when she was found. Adams and his group only arrived in New York the other day. This is what brought them here, I'm sure of it."

"So," she said. "What now? Do we tell the police, or let these people from Boston deal with it?"

"We can't go to the police," he said, tucking the documents away into their folders. "They'd never believe us. Maybe Adams can handle this, but I still want to know what's going on."

Nathan considered Miranda Grange's address on the autopsy report. He knew the place. It was a tenement-style apartment building on the Upper West Side, close to Harlem. "You should get back to work before you're missed." Cynthia, a medical examiner, put her job at risk every time she helped him. "Thank you for this, Cynthia, seriously."

She nodded and stood with him. "I should be able to get access to Miranda Grange's effects. Maybe I can find out what's being overlooked by the police, and why."

After Cynthia left to go back to work, Nathan returned to his car and made his way to Miranda Grange's apartment building.

He managed to find parking two blocks away from the place. That was good, since he didn't want his car too close to the building. He had taken sick days to investigate cases before and never been caught, but breaking into private property was a little more serious.

He took a walk around the area, taking in details of the people in the neighborhood, the faces which seemed to haunt the same places, and noting the layout of the buildings.

Miranda Grange's name was scribbled in blue pen on a row of doorbells on the porch, next to the mailboxes. *No new tenant yet.* The police would want her apartment left vacant until the investigation into her death was completed. Her place was on the sixth floor. He headed to the elevator.

Paint flaked away from the old plaster, and patches of mold had grown in lines where water pipes lay behind the walls. Stale air filled the halls. Nathan reached Miranda's door and tried the handle. It was locked. He looked out the window at the end of the hall, mentally noting where the room was located.

Nathan could visualize places and things that he'd only seen briefly. Sometimes he could pick out details he hadn't consciously noticed. With a quick scan of the building's exterior, he would now be able to locate Miranda's room from the outside.

He left the building and walked to his car. The rational part of his brain said to go home, have a beer, and watch a movie. Forget all of this. It had nothing to do with him, right? This wasn't like following a missing persons case in the news and sending anonymous tips to the police. If he kept investigating these murders, believing real-life monsters were behind it all, he could lose Laura, his job, or even his life.

But the idea of being on the threshold of a hidden world where vampires walked the night was intoxicating. Nathan was convinced that his dreams held unspoken truths. He just had to figure out what they were.

His two most vivid dreams were the one in which he was wearing ancient Roman amour, and the one where he tried to kill the vampire Eli. In both dreams, he had been killed by his opponent. Waking from them left Nathan hollow; he ached to know what they meant.

Nathan's father called as he was sitting in his car. The sun was beginning to set.

"How soon can you get to the corner of West 50th and 10th Avenue?"

Nathan started the engine. "Traffic's not great but I can get there soon enough. Hang on, West 50th and 10th? That's in Hell's Kitchen."

"That's where the surprise is."

"I don't like you wandering around there on your own this late, Dad."

The Kitchen had been cleaned up a lot from its former gangland days, but it was also a hotspot for the kinds of missing persons reports and unexplained animal attacks Nathan had investigated.

"Don't worry about me, son. I know my way around a rough street or two."

Nathan drove as fast as he could get away with, finally rounding the turn onto 10th Avenue. Up ahead, Mike waved him down from the sidewalk.

Nathan pulled over and climbed out of the car, pausing to put some coins in a parking meter. "So, what's this surprise?"

Mike smiled. "You're standing next to it, son."

He looked at the building behind his dad. A boarded-up shop front between a dry cleaner and a deli advertising a special offer on meatball subs. A sign of some sort had once hung over the door, but the paint had peeled away so only half the letters remained. Nathan could make out the word "bar."

"I don't get it," he said. "You bought this?"

Mike shrugged. "Nah, course not, I rented it. The lease is paid up for a full year. Fully licensed premises, all four stories. Second floor's already converted for use. Got a cellar, too. Nice little garden and parking lot tucked away in the back."

"Lease?"

"Yup, signed it today." He held up a key. "Wanna see inside?"

Nathan held up a hand. "You're going to run a bar?"

Mike unlocked the door and pushed it open. "Not on my own. I was talking to an old firefighter buddy. He's got a kid who's been managing this place down in Jersey for about three years now. He wants to get some work in Manhattan. Come on in. It's cold outside."

Nathan stepped into the darkened old bar. He shivered and rubbed his arms. "Not much better inside, Dad." He found a light switch and flicked it, but nothing happened.

"There're some things to get fixed up. Need the power turned back on, some renovations."

Mike took a small flashlight from his jacket pocket and turned it on, shining it around the main room. A pale layer of dust covered everything. The place was littered with empty bottles, upturned or broken tables and chairs, not to mention broken beams hanging down from the ceiling above the bar itself.

"You sure it isn't condemned?" Nathan tried to lift an old chair, but a loose nail came away and the pieces fell to the floor, sending up a cloud of choking dust.

"Now don't you go nay saying, son," Mike said. "I thought this through. I've wanted a place like this for a long time. I've got the money, and I may as well do it while I've still got the years left to enjoy it. Should be able to get it fixed up in a couple of months then arrange a big opening night. Maybe get in a few music acts, you know?"

Nathan wiped dust from his face and clothes. "I don't want to see you getting in over your head. There's a lot of damage here, and the neighborhood—"

"Aw, now don't go talking like that. The neighborhood's not so bad. And the load-bearing walls are strong." He slapped a wall firmly with his free hand. "Sure, it's got a history; it used to be a gang hangout years ago. But I think it deserves a second chance."

Mike sat down on a rickety stool and looked around the room, a glimmer of excitement in his tired eyes. "The outside's a bit rough and worn, but it wants to be used again. It ought to be doing something good, the way this world is, you know?"

Nathan nodded. "Yeah." He sat next to his father, making sure his stool wasn't about to collapse under him. "Got a name yet?"

"I have a few ideas."

"Tell you what, Dad, let's get something to eat and we can talk about it. I've been craving a meatball sub since we got here."

They went next door to the deli and ordered a couple of sandwiches and Cokes. They talked about bar names and the son of Mike's old friend who would be helping to run the place. It was good to see his dad so eager about this. As hard as it had been for Mike to be forced into retirement, losing his wife had been worse. Nathan had missed seeing that bright glint in his dad's eyes.

After dropping Mike off at home, Nathan parked his car back near Miranda Grange's apartment and went for another long walk to pass some time. After ten o'clock, when it had long since become dark, he made his way back to the apartment.

Scaling the fire escape without drawing too much attention was easy enough. Miranda's apartment looked out into a quiet alleyway around the back of the building. Nathan knelt next to the window of the apartment and set his bag down before taking off his jacket. A quick glance around the window and surrounding wall left him confident there was no alarm. He held the jacket against the glass and took a deep breath. He broke the window with a hard slam from his elbow. The jacket muffled the sound and stopped him from being cut by the pieces. *No turning back now.*

He ducked under the window frame and climbed inside. The main room consisted of a small sitting area with a sofa and a couple of armchairs around a coffee table covered with gossip magazines. A framed photograph lay face-down on top of a television set in the corner. He pulled on a pair of leather gloves and took out his flashlight to begin looking around.

The photo frame was empty. Nathan leafed through the magazines and found a few tabloids with different articles circled in red tucked underneath them. Most of the stories were about unusual or violent deaths. He had followed up on some of the same news events himself.

As he leafed through the documents he began to understand Miranda. She, like him, had delved into the dark secrets of New York. Would he end up the way she had? Dying scared and alone?

In front of another window there was a modest computer desk. Patches in the light layer of dust suggested a laptop had once sat there. CD holders sat empty, and an Internet cable lay forgotten on the floor. Someone had been here already.

The kitchenette in the corner was stocked with cheap microwave meals and soft drinks. A half-finished bottle of vodka sat next to the kettle, and there were empty bottles in the trash along with boxes from a Chinese restaurant.

Nathan found some utility bills near the door and a receipt from the landlord for a year's rent in advance, dated from three months earlier. *Who pays up a year's rent in advance and then lives on cheap takeaways and TV dinners?* With that kind of money to spare why choose to live in a small apartment in a bad neighborhood?

The bedroom was neatly kept. There were some clothes in the wardrobe, underwear in drawers, and basic cosmetics on a small dresser. The carpet under the bed was scuffed and worn, like something heavy had been regularly slid out from under it and back again.

In the bathroom's medicine cabinet there was a selection of painkillers and sleeping pills. Nathan found a well-stocked first aid kit on the floor.

Whoever had been here had hardly taken anything. No personal effects, no valuables. The front door hadn't been forced open, and apart from his own handiwork, Nathan could see no other signs of forced entry.

He sat on the sofa and leaned forward. Adams and his group would have had time to get word of Miranda's death, arrive in New York, and investigate her apartment. If they were next of kin, why hadn't they claimed her body? And why wouldn't the landlord have them take the rest of Miranda's things? All they took from her apartment was her computer and a photograph. That didn't make sense.

Unless they broke in? Assuming one of them knew how to pick a lock—not an unreasonable skill for these people to have—they could have been here and left without anyone knowing.

Odds were good that the photograph had purely sentimental value. There weren't any others in the apartment. It was likely that Miranda kept all her findings stored on her computer. So the vampire killers wanted her notes.

But if they got them, what are they doing now? And why were they in the building where she was found?

Nathan thought back to the file on Miranda. She'd been found on the roof of the building, and that was where Adams had said he and the others had been.

The woman with Adams had talked about some kind of creature—not the vampires—which had dropped its victim onto the street. Perhaps they were hunting the thing that had killed Miranda?

Nathan thought he heard something creaking. He shook his head and ignored it. He was in an old building full of tenants. There were bound to be sounds coming from somewhere. Still, he'd learned pretty much all he could. He decided he'd have to take a look at where Miranda was killed, maybe see if he could figure out where to find her killer. If it was some kind of predator that slept for a decade at a time, waking up to feed, it might have a nest or lair close by.

Hell, it was as good a theory as any.

He climbed back out onto the fire escape and froze. Something snarled above him. He looked up in time to see a person drop down and land on the rail of the fire escape, blocking his way to the steps down. In the dim light he recognized the vampire whose nose he'd broken the night before.

"Look at this," he growled, perched on the rail like a cat. "Mr. Flashlight."

Nathan turned to climb to the next level, but another person dropped to the grate above him. It was Eli.

"Adams shouldn't be sending kids to do grown-ups' work, should he, Gideon?"

The darker-haired vampire chuckled.

"All alone, this time? Do me a favor." Eli flashed his teeth and his eyes turned the color of putrid milk. "Run. It's much more fun."

Chapter Five

NATHAN VAULTED OVER THE RAILING AND DROPPED, catching the rail one level down with his right arm. He wrenched his shoulder and almost fell the rest of the way, but managed to hang on and pull himself over the rail. He fled down the fire escape to the street.

Gideon leaped from the fire escape and landed in front of Nathan, stopping him in his tracks. The vampire stood from his crouched landing as if it had been only a three foot drop instead of thirty. Nathan turned and ran the opposite way, deeper into the back alleys. Gideon was fast behind him and Eli dropped down to join the chase. Nathan slowed and whipped his flashlight around, smashing the end into Gideon's face. There was a crunch and a spray of blood as Gideon stumbled to the ground holding his nose. Pulling his injured partner up by the collar, Eli snarled something unintelligible. Nathan turned and kept running.

They chased him down the dark alleys between the buildings, their growls and shouts urging him on. He didn't scream or cry for help. He just ran.

Nathan made it out through the long alleyway. He sprinted into oncoming traffic, causing one car to swerve into another and almost getting hit by a passing taxi cab. The sounds of the city quickly drowned out those of his pursuers.

He reached Riverside Drive and tumbled over a fence into some bushes, scratching his face and hands. After scrambling to his feet and hurrying across the street, Nathan vaulted over another fence into Riverside Park, looking out across the Hudson River. Only a few stray strands of light filtered through the trees, leaving him all but blind. He stopped and leaned on a tree to catch his breath, swallowing in deep gulps of air. He listened for his pursuers.

Nothing.

Then he heard the dull thud of boots on soft earth. They were still behind him. He took off again but they were closing in. Nathan reached into his bag and pulled out his claw hammer. With that in one hand and his flashlight in the other, he prepared to defend himself.

Eli caught up first. The two leaped over a park bench and Eli threw himself against Nathan, who rolled with the fall. Nathan swung the hammer at Eli's knee, catching it with a glancing blow. He followed up and struck him in the hip with his flashlight, throwing the vampire off balance. Nathan pushed up and kept running, though his lungs were heaving and his leg muscles burned.

The delay was enough for Gideon to reach him. Both vampires were right behind him and while Nathan felt his vision begin to blur, his legs and lungs ready to give up on him, they seemed to be managing just fine.

Nathan saw a light up ahead, coming from a two-story cottage, right in the middle of the park. The door opened and a thin man with a goatee and dark hair hanging over his eyes stepped into view.

Nathan cried out. "Help!"

He stumbled and one of the vampires fell onto him, clawing at his back. Nathan wriggled out of the strap of his sports bag. He glanced back and saw Gideon snarl as he raked thick black claws across his shoulder. Nathan pulled himself out from under Gideon, repeating his cries for help.

"Say sanctuary," the thin man said.

"What?" Nathan was about ten feet from the door. He stopped to try and stand. That was a mistake.

Eli pounced, launching himself through the air and smashing into him, wrapping his arms around him. Nathan's chin hit the ground and Eli pinned him. With no leverage, and his body weak from fatigue, Nathan was unable to free himself.

"Say sanctuary," the thin man said again, calmly. "If you want to live, say it."

Eli snarled behind Nathan's ear.

"Sanctuary!" Nathan's strength gave out with that last scream.

Eli froze. Everything was quiet for several seconds, before Eli growled, "This isn't your business, Roland. Dorian wants him."

The thin man lit a cigarette and took a slow drag. "This man has claimed sanctuary on my territory. Rules are rules. You break sanctuary here and Dorian can send someone to collect what's left."

Nathan kept still while the two men talked. Eli snarled before letting him up. He ran to the door, almost falling into the cottage as Roland stepped aside.

Gideon emptied Nathan's sports bag out onto the ground. "It's not here," he said. "He's got nothing."

Eli turned and shouted something in a language Nathan didn't understand. "Where is it?" He looked back to Nathan. "Where's the woman's information?"

"I don't know what you're talking about," Nathan replied between deep breaths. "I didn't find anything."

Eli stepped forward while Gideon continued going through Nathan's things, including his camera, notepad, and his cell phone. "You tell Adams to get back where he belongs, got it?"

"I'm not with Adams." Nathan's voice shook.

"Then I guess we'll be seeing more of each other." Eli gave an exaggerated bow to Nathan and Roland. "Be seeing you. Come on, Gideon. Let this guy go. He's nobody."

Gideon kicked the contents of Nathan's bag a few times and the two walked away.

Roland shut the door and Nathan collapsed against the wall, holding his head in his hands.

"Coffee?" Roland asked.

Nathan pulled himself up and followed Roland into the modest kitchen. He sat down at the simple wooden table and Roland set a mug of steaming coffee down in front of him.

It helped steady Nathan's nerves a little. He spooned sugar into the mug, something he hadn't done since college. The whole cottage had a rustic feel, definitely out of place in Manhattan. Nathan felt a dreamlike sense of his surroundings, as though he'd stepped out of his own time.

"Feeling better?" Roland asked, at last. He stubbed out his cigarette and offered Nathan one from a pack. He declined.

"I think so," Nathan said. "Little bit of pain, though."

Roland nodded. "Looks like they roughed you up a bit, all right. You want me to take a look? Adrenaline's a pal, but it'll wear off soon."

Nathan agreed and removed his sweater. His right arm hurt where he'd caught the metal railings. A large bruise formed close to his elbow.

Roland checked him over quickly. "Some cuts and bruises," he said, getting an old-fashioned doctor's bag from a cabinet. "Nothing serious. Gideon's claws didn't go too deep, so we can use some steri-strips instead of a suture. You have a girl?"

Nathan nodded. "Yeah, her name's Laura."

Roland gave a slow nod. "Cool. Chicks dig scars. Not sure how much of a scar this'll leave, but you might be lucky."

"I don't feel lucky."

"Of course not. You just got your ass kicked." Roland applied some antiseptic to a cotton pad and cleaned the three marks where Gideon's claws had broken the skin on his shoulder. "You should consider heavier layers for this game, kid. Cotton won't do a damn thing. How long you been in the trade?"

"Trade?" Nathan winced. The antiseptic stung, and Roland wasn't exactly being gentle.

"Yeah," Roland said. "The trade." He sniffed a little. "You don't know what that means, do you?"

Nathan shook his head. "Should I?"

"Damn." Roland placed some steri-strips over the wounds and stuck a cotton pad over them with some surgical tape to keep them clean. "Right, time for a rookie-talk. Been a while."

Roland handed the antiseptic solution to Nathan along with some cotton pads to let him clean the rest of his cuts. He sat down again and lit another cigarette.

"The trade is what we do, okay? If you're in the trade, you know that things aren't like they say they are on the morning news. Vampires, witches, ghosts, magic, demons, it's all real. Or close enough to real, anyway. Normal people live their lives in their quiet little worlds, happily unaware that their neighbor is a necromancer or that bum who asked them for change needs to eat their heart to live another hundred years. You and me, we're different. People like us see the world the way it really is. Some of us are psychic, some dabble in magic, and some use past-life memories to see beyond the mundane. With me so far?"

Nathan nodded, silently cleaning his bloodied chin.

"Good. Now, this is important. In this city, the big man is Dorian. Those two vampire low-lives work for him."

"Is Dorian a vampire?"

"No." Roland shook his head. "He's something else. He, and others like him, have used magic to stop themselves from aging. Forever. He's a lord of the Council of Chains. Mortals who seek immortality."

"Council of Chains?" Nathan raised an eyebrow.

Roland nodded. "Yeah, some party line about chaining the soul to the body, chains setting you free from death, that kind of ironic bullshit. Dorian runs this town, and people like you aren't exactly welcome."

"What do you mean, like me?" Nathan finished up with the antiseptic and pulled his sweater back on.

"People who go poking around where they're not wanted, kid. You want to survive in this big bad wolf of a city, you've got two choices. Either go home and forget everything or learn to look after yourself."

Nathan rubbed his face and leaned back in the chair. "Why are you telling me all this?"

Roland got up to make more coffee. "You asked for sanctuary. That's a sacred thing, even to the likes of Dorian. I'm obliged to offer you shelter and protection. I figured I'd offer a bit of free advice, too."

"So anytime anyone is asked for shelter, they and their, uh, guests are safe from harm?"

"Oh, gods, no," Roland laughed. "I've sworn the Oath of Sanctuary. Means I'm neutral in any conflicts that crop up. I can't get involved, and I can't be touched. Same with anyone who's under my protection. So long as you're here, you're safe."

"And when I leave?" Nathan didn't like the idea of Eli and Gideon waiting for him to walk out the door.

"You've got an hour after leaving my home before anything in the city can touch you. Don't worry. Most of us, even mortals in the know, gain a sense of these things as time goes on. Most people block out that extra sense, but when you're in the trade it all comes back. Think of it as walking around with a big neon 'don't fuck with me' sign over your head." Roland set another hot mug of coffee down in front of Nathan. "Drink up."

"Has anyone ever broken the rule?" Nathan asked. "You know, killed someone under sanctuary?"

Roland stared into his mug for a moment. His eyes looked old and grey, tired. "Yeah. It's happened. There are … consequences." He looked up. "You're best not messing with that kind of power. Ancient oaths and rites have a strength that can level cities, if they're pushed."

Nathan took a scalding mouthful of coffee. "I've got a lot of questions."

Roland nodded. "I'll bet. But you should know, under the Oath of Sanctuary, if anyone asks me what I've told you, I have to tell them. So watch your words, okay?"

Nathan thought about that for a while before saying anything. His mind buzzed with questions, most of which he was afraid to ask.

"Okay," he said at last. "Dorian's the big bad guy. Who're the good guys? Adams and his people?"

Shaking his head, Roland wrinkled his nose. "Heh, no. Damn. Is Adams back in town? Shit."

"So he's a bad guy?"

"No. But I wouldn't exactly call him a hero, either. He's a pragmatist, and a bit of an extremist. He's a reborn." Roland seemed to predict Nathan's next question and began to explain. "The reborn are people who remember their past lives. Well, more than that. See, pretty much every sorry soul on the planet has been here at least once before. Some people get flashes of past lives, or find that they can pick up certain skills more easily than others. All of that is tapping into lost memories. Reborn are better at it than most. They've lived more lives, and from a young age they have strange dreams or master new talents quickly. It really kicks off near the end of the teenage years. By the time they're thirty, most reborn can remember centuries of lives they once had. Some have souls going back beyond recorded mundane history."

Nathan nodded slowly, taking it all in. He started putting the pieces together in his mind.

"Now, the reborn are a fairly loose organization of people. More like a bunch of folks with a common belief or spirituality than anything else. But they don't get along with the Council of Chains. The two have been at each others' throats for longer than I can remember, and I can remember a hell of a lot."

Nathan raised an eyebrow as a thought came to mind. "The reborn see life and death as an eternal cycle. Something sacred. The Council defies the natural order by preventing their own deaths."

Roland paused, his cigarette hanging limply from his lips. "Yeah, actually." He took a puff and held the cigarette between his fingers. "The reborn see the Council as selfish monsters, and the Council think the reborns' stories about a reincarnated soul still being the same person are just dogma."

Nathan's eyes met Roland's, and for a moment the older man's face lifted. "But why?" Nathan asked. "If reincarnation is real, why all the conflict?"

"Because no one's really sure who's right," Roland said. "People in the Council admit that they have memories of a life that's not their own, but no one really knows what happens after you die, between the points of death and rebirth. Some say the soul stays the same, always learning and growing in power as it remembers. There are a lot of reborn who're smarter, stronger, and faster than they ought to be, which fits that. But there's a case to be made that, while you get memories of a past life, they're just that. Memories. Nothing more. You just get details and knowledge. Some say when you die, the person you were is lost forever, and that scares the shit out of people like the Council; they dabble in dark arts, becoming vampires, revenants, liches, anything they can do to ward off death."

"So this Dorian, he's just a man?"

Roland laughed. "You're gonna have a fun time in this town, I can tell. No, Dorian got into some seriously dark shit. No one's really sure of all the details, but he got a pretty good deal, far as I can tell. He gets eternal life, health and youth, plus a whole lot of arcane knowledge and other neat little superpowers; though he can be killed. But don't go getting any ideas. Dorian's damn smart. You don't get to live as long as him without learning how to take anyone who gets in your way and put them in the ground."

"Which are you?"

"Let's just say that Dorian wouldn't shed a tear for me, if you know what I mean."

Nathan looked around the room at Roland's collection of old photographs and books. "You said that sometimes reborn have dreams about past lives, right?"

Roland nodded.

"I think I've had some. A lot, even."

Roland urged him to continue with a circle of his hand.

"I've had dreams about being ... different people. A Roman soldier, a sailor, a highwayman."

"How often?"

"Almost every night. As long as I can remember."

He sniffed, looking Nathan up and down. "Long time to have the dreams and not realize what's going on. You're afraid, huh?"

"No, I'm, not—"

"Sure you are," Roland cut across. "I was afraid when I first remembered. It's natural. But if you're done being a wuss about it, maybe you should man up a bit and start facing your memories."

"I don't think I know how." Nathan slumped in his chair.

"Cut the lost lamb act before I give you your second ass-kicking of the night." Roland crushed his cigarette out. "It's easy. Next time you feel the memory coming on, whether you're dreaming or you're awake—and believe me, you'll get them when you're awake—don't resist it. Dive right in. Give in to the thoughts and feelings. It's easier to do with dreams, but the memories you get when you're awake are stronger. If you can unlock those, you'll remember all kinds of stuff. How to fight, how to ride a horse, how to make a chambermaid curl her toes. . . ."

Roland's expression drifted into a dreamy smile. He shook his head and turned his attention back to Nathan. "Sorry about that."

Nathan shrugged, daring to laugh a little. "It's okay."

"Oh, one more thing. You've stumbled into this on your own, so as far as Dorian and Adams will be concerned, you're not affiliated with anybody. You're under no one's command, but you're under no one's protection. You tell anyone about what's really going on, you bring them into our world, and they're your responsibility until they can defend themselves, got it?"

Nathan nodded. "Sure, that's okay. I mean, I haven't really . . . oh, God." He ran to the door.

Cynthia.

Nathan left Roland, hurried to his car and prayed he'd get there on time.

Chapter Six

Cadence flashed her ID badge as they passed the last security guard. It was a pretty simple mock-up—there hadn't been time to make a decent forgery—but it did the job when used alongside a confident stride and two companions, all dressed like doctors. They managed a good show of it, even though Lane looked more like a retired cage fighter than a medical professional, and Adams habitually scanned every door and hallway they passed.

Cadence opened the door into the morgue. Just one person, also in a lab coat, sat with his back to them working at a computer in the corner. She glanced up at the room's security camera and sent a small wave of energy through her fingertips. She heard a low fizzle and the little red light on the camera went out. She nodded to Lane, who stepped quickly up to the doctor.

Lane pulled a taser from under his coat and fired. The barbs struck the doctor in the back and he convulsed before collapsing to the ground. Jim restrained him with duct tape while Adams sat at the computer and went to work.

"Drawer four," he said.

Cadence pulled open drawer number four on the wall of freezer units. She unzipped the bag inside. Miranda's face was so twisted it was barely recognizable. She must have been in great pain. Cadence closed her eyes and counted slowly to three, steadying herself. There was too much work to do for her to lose it.

She checked Miranda for wounds, anything to indicate how she had been killed, but found none. Whatever had killed Miranda had left her body largely unharmed, except for some small cuts on the arms and some light bruising on the shoulder and hips. Almost as if something held her down. There was mud caked under her broken fingernails. Whatever happened, she had definitely fought back.

"They found her equipment with her," Adams said. "Most of it's been taken by the police as evidence. Except for a flash drive which is still here. A Dr. Cynthia Keller requisitioned it."

"Anything on cause of death?" Cadence asked.

"Heart failure. You *can* tell me more than that, right?"

Cadence held her hand over Miranda's chest and closed her eyes. A side effect of lifetimes spent studying the magical arts was the ability to sense the way magical energy interacted with and flowed through the environment. Dead bodies held on to some residual energy from the soul after it departed.

Except Miranda didn't.

She was empty. *How?* Even inanimate objects had essence flowing inside them. There should have been something left behind when Miranda was killed. Instead, it was as though something had sucked every last bit of life from her.

"Whenever you're ready, Cadence."

Why wouldn't he let her work? "I don't understand it. There's nothing left. Her essence has been completely sucked out."

"That's not possible. Check again."

"I don't need to, I know what I felt."

"Just do it!"

Cadence was about to yell back, but a pulse of magical energy blew through her. Her throat caught as though she were about to gag. The lights flickered and the screen on the office computer blinked for a second.

What was that?

Cynthia tapped the keys while her monitor had a brief electric spasm. It only lasted for a second or so, but the software took a little longer to respond. Technology was dumbfounding. She could talk to her aunt in Germany any time she wanted, but they still couldn't make a word processor that worked when she was in a hurry.

She hated staying late but Nathan was on to something. Although it was a risk, she'd managed to get access to Miranda Grange's body and personal effects. Among the possessions had been a flash drive containing photographs and notes which Cynthia was currently reviewing on her office computer. The photographs were mostly of old buildings and some people she'd seemed to be tracking. The notes were far more interesting. Miranda was looking for something, some creature or other. She had typed in some kind of shorthand or code that was difficult to decipher. Mostly, she made reference to something she called "the eater," which she'd spent several months trying to find.

As soon as Nathan saw this, there would be no stopping him. He would dive right in, ready to save the day. Of course he wouldn't tell Laura, or any of their other friends. Not that they'd believe him. Cynthia barely believed it herself, but she and Nathan had found enough mysteries to give her an open mind about things. This was different, though. This was real and happening right now. The mere promise of the answers Miranda's notes offered would be a drug to Nathan.

She had to watch his back for him. No one else would.

There was a knock and Cynthia's office door opened. A man in a suit with hair shaved short to hide a receding hairline stepped inside, adjusting a pair of glasses on his nose. Two other men walked behind him. One was scruffy, with a beaten jacket and dark hair sticking up in several places. The other was lean and thin, with blonde hair tied into a ponytail. Cynthia recognized them from the Miranda Grange pictures.

"I'm sorry," she said. "I don't believe we have an appointment, I—"

The suited man raised a single finger to silence her. "Ms. Keller, I understand you're doing some work on the death of Miranda Grange?"

"I'm afraid I can't discuss my case work, Mr...?"

"Ah," he said. "How rude of me." He extended a hand. "I am Jonah Creek. My associates and I would like to ask some questions."

"Look, Mr. Creek, I'm really sorry, but I am quite busy, and I'm sure you can appreciate the confidentiality."

"Confidentiality?" Creek almost sang the word. "I doubt that was such an issue when you were sharing your information with Mr. Shepherd."

Her face fell. "What?"

"Nathan Shepherd." Creek gave a smooth practiced smile, looking around the room, taking apparent care not to touch anything. "You two have been noticed." He checked her computer monitor, then under her desk. "Gideon, the flash drive here. Take it and destroy this computer."

Cynthia swallowed back a cry of fear. "I don't want trouble. Just take what you want and go. Please."

Creek's lips curled in a lopsided smile. "Yes, I think that we shall. Eli?"

The other man was suddenly behind Cynthia. She spun and backed away, walking into her desk. Gideon put the flash drive in his pocket and lifted the PC tower before smashing it down on the monitor and tearing it apart with his hands.

Eli backed Cynthia against the desk. "Should I hurt her, break her, or kill her?"

Creek licked his lips. "Hurt her. A lot."

Cynthia shook as Eli reached for her. She screamed, but no one came to help.

Nathan drove his car hard through the streets. He'd been ticketed for not keeping the parking meter paid up, but that was far from his thoughts right now. The Chief Medical Examiner's Office loomed up ahead. He skidded into a stop across two parking spaces and ran inside, pushing past people as he did.

A burly security guard stood in his way and held up his hands. "Sir, stop, please. I can't let you past here without a visitor's pass."

"I'm looking for Dr. Keller. She's a friend. Can you see if she's in her office?"

The guard nodded and led Nathan over to the reception desk. "No problem, sir. Just wait here and I'll see."

He lifted the receiver and pressed a button for an internal line. Nathan shifted his feet while they waited for an answer. *She'll be fine, she'll be fine.*

The guard frowned and hung up the phone. "There's no answer. She's still checked in, though. It's possible she's in the lab."

"I need to see her!"

The guard stepped back in front of Nathan. "Sir, I'll ask you once more to calm down, or I'll have to escort you from the premises."

Three men left an elevator down the hall. The first was a pasty-looking man in a grey suit and glasses, with close-shaved hair receding away from his forehead. Behind him, Nathan recognized Eli and Gideon. His heart raced as they walked toward him. The man in the grey suit walked by without looking at him, but Eli flashed a grin and winked. Nathan turned to watch them leave and felt a sickening knot grow in his stomach.

Nathan rushed past the security guard. Someone in a white lab coat stepped into the elevator and the doors slid shut. Nathan shouted at the lab worker in vain and hit the door with his fist. With the security guard close behind him, Nathan ran for the emergency stairs. When he reached Cynthia's floor, he hurried to her office, finding the door ajar.

Nathan's knees nearly gave out under him when he looked inside. Cynthia lay on the floor in a bloody heap. Her clothing had been torn and her face was swollen. Nathan knelt next to her, gently touching her hand. "Cynthia?" The security guard came to a stop right behind him, grabbing hold of his shoulders.

"Nath-an." Her voice was weak, barely above a whisper. She opened her left eye, the right was swollen shut. The skin had been broken on her eye socket and cheekbone. Blood dripped from her mouth as she tried to speak.

Nathan shook off the guard's grip, leaving him gawking in shock, and looked around the room, taking in details. Framed certificates had been knocked from the wall, breaking the glass. Her desk was a mess and her computer had been torn apart.

"Eli … Creek …" With effort, Cynthia tried to speak.

Creek must have been the name of the man in the suit. Nathan used the damage in the room to construct mental images of what had happened in his mind, picturing Eli throwing her around the room, knocking books from the splintered shelf to one side, smashing her face against the wall, cutting her on the glass from the certificate frames. Kicking her. Beating her.

"Jesus." The security guard's voice shook. "What the hell happened?"

Nathan barked out instructions. "Get help, she needs a doctor, now! And call the police!"

The guard nodded and left.

Nathan, remembering how Adams had checked him for bite marks when he'd saved him from Eli, checked Cynthia's throat and wrists, but found nothing. Most of the damage looked like blunt force.

"Cynthia." He pulled away hair stuck to her face with blood. "I'm here, you're okay. What happened? What did they want?"

"Miranda … had notes…" She was having trouble staying conscious. Nathan tried stroking her face and shaking her lightly to keep her awake. "She … flash drive. They got the…"

Nathan nodded, helping sit Cynthia up. "Okay, they got the flash drive, that's okay. You're going to be all right, I promise."

"No." Cynthia tried to shake her head, but began to gag, as though she were about to vomit. She didn't, but her head fell back. Nathan caught it and shifted so she could lie against him.

"It's not your fault. I'm sorry, Cynthia, I shouldn't have got you involved."

"Nathan you … damn it … listen…" She fumbled at her pants pocket, but her fingers were twisted all wrong and she couldn't move them.

Nathan looked down. "You've got something you want to show me?" She nodded slightly.

Hesitating briefly, Nathan reached into her pocket. "Sorry," he said, sure that he saw her roll her good eye. Inside her pocket he felt something small, about the shape and size of a cigarette lighter. He took it out. *Another flash drive?* She had made a copy.

Cynthia's head rolled back. Nathan had no chance to ask her about it. He tried to keep her awake by saying her name over and over until a doctor arrived.

The office became a swarm of confusion and motion. An ambulance crew moved Cynthia downstairs. Nathan stayed with her, riding along in the ambulance. The paramedics confirmed she had a concussion and asked him to keep talking to her to keep her awake on the way to the hospital. He tried to make as much casual conversation as he could manage, and found himself talking about Laura.

"I need to fix things, Cynthia. When all this is over and we get back to normal, I'm going to set everything right. Look what happened to you. This is my fault. I need to grow up, marry Laura and start a family, like my dad wants. I don't want to see people I care about get hurt."

He looked down at Cynthia. She was smiling. "She'll probably want you as her maid of honor."

"Nice," Cynthia murmured.

"That went well," Cadence said as she ducked into the car. Lane revved the engine to life and pulled away from the building.

Cadence closed her eyes and sent her senses out into the surrounding energy fields. The pulse she'd felt had given off no overt energy. It was more like a sudden dulling of the senses. She figured it was some kind of a veil, a spell designed to hide the caster from being seen or heard. But she hadn't had a chance to try and work out more than that before people started running through the halls shouting about a break-in.

Lane turned on his police scanner and a woman's voice came out over it. There'd been an assault on someone in the building. There wasn't a lot of information available, but paramedics had been called.

"Any idea what that was?" Adams asked.

Cadence rested back in her seat. "Not at that range. The caster was too far from me. And he was good. The spell went up quick. I'm thinking some kind of veil. Probably whoever committed the assault."

Lane was staring ahead. "What now?"

Adams shrugged. "We need to let the heat die down before we try to find Miranda's notes again. If this were fifteen years ago, I could've called in a favor with the cops."

"It's not fifteen years ago," Lane said. "Damn mess. We left evidence behind us. We didn't get all the security cameras. We're compromised. Don't even know what Miranda found here or what killed her."

"I imagine that whatever Miranda found was the thing that killed her," Cadence said. "There aren't many things that'll do that to a person."

Lane grimaced. She felt bad for him. He and Miranda both lost their families in the war. It was only natural they would hook up. It hadn't taken Lane and Miranda long to figure out they'd been together in past lives. There was work to be done, though. They needed to keep focused.

"We need someone with local knowledge," Cadence said. "We don't know the territory, and we shouldn't be here without permission. If the Council finds us, they'll claim right of execution."

"I know what you're thinking," Adams said. "But that Shepherd kid's not ready for this."

"He's the first native New York reborn we've heard of in almost twenty years," she said. "For all we know, there are others. If so, they're exempt from the treaty. They can offer us sanctuary and protection."

"And he might just be one man," Adams said. "One man, on his own, finding all of this out for the first time. We don't have time to babysit him."

He sighed, looking at Cadence in the rear-view mirror. "When this is over, we can see if he wants to come back with us, learn what he needs to know. Then, maybe, we can think about shaking things up in this town." He checked his pistol, switching off the safety and re-holstering it under his arm. "For now, we're here to find out what Miranda learned."

The ambulance brought them to the New York Downtown Hospital. It was the only emergency hospital on the south of Manhattan. It was also where Laura worked. She was on duty when the paramedics wheeled Cynthia in on a gurney.

"Good God." Laura checked Cynthia over, asking her to confirm if she could feel pressure or pain at various places on her body.

Cynthia responded with small nods or a shake of her head.

"Multiple trauma points," Laura said. "Minor lacerations, possible broken bones or fractures."

She turned to a nurse. "Get this woman prepped for X-ray and put her on a light morphine IV. We'll need the minor wounds dressed. I'll do the sutures myself."

The nurse nodded and responded in the affirmative before taking Cynthia away.

Laura turned to Nathan and fixed him with a glare. "What the hell happened?"

"I'm not sure. She was helping me look into some things and," he shook his head. "You'd never believe me."

Laura folded her arms. "Try me."

"I think there's a two-hundred-year-old monster killing people."

She blinked. "Are you serious?"

He didn't speak.

Laura leaned in closer. She sniffed. Nathan frowned. Was she smelling his breath?

"All right, I don't care what's going on between you and Cynthia, but I don't have time for this bullshit."

"Look, Laura. I've found things. You wouldn't believe what I've learned."

"You're right," she said. "I wouldn't. And I don't have time to discuss this with you now. Cynthia is hurt, and it's my job to make her better. We can talk about how it happened later."

She walked away and Nathan leaned against the wall, wondering what he'd gotten himself into.

"Nathan!" A shout came from down the hospital corridor. Nathan looked up from his Styrofoam coffee cup and saw Ben walking with a purpose; strong, sharp movements, his work boots clumping down on the tiles.

Ben was a large man with thick shovels for hands and dark, curly hair atop a thick brick of a head. His brow sloped over a strong, grizzled face; all stubble and sun tan wrapped around a lantern-jaw. He was Nathan's oldest friend. Along with Cynthia and Laura, they had been inseparable back in college.

He stepped up to Nathan, frowning. "Laura called. What's going on?"

Nathan explained more or less what had happened over the last two days. Ben leaned back on the bench next to him and blew out a long breath.

"What you're talking about isn't possible."

"I know. What more do you want me to say?"

"I just need a minute to get my head around it." He rubbed his face in his hands. "How long have you and Cynthia been doing this?"

"About two years, on and off. But it was just a hobby, really. We'd get together and read blogs about ghosts and legends, looking up all kinds of strange stories from around New York. Then, a year or so ago, things got serious."

"Whoa." He gripped Nathan's arm, probably tighter than he'd intended. It hurt a little. "You mean you and Cynthia?"

Nathan pulled away. "No, of course not. I'd never do that to Laura. I know we're going through a rough spot but come on."

He and Cynthia had gone out a couple of times back in college, before he and Laura got together, but there was nothing romantic between them now.

Ben sat back. His gaze wandered around the hall.

"The stuff we were into got serious." Nathan clasped his hands together, but it didn't stop them from shaking. "There was a missing persons case on the news. A girl disappeared one night in Central Park, near where there had been some strange animal attacks reported. The police had no leads. I took Cynthia with me one night and we checked out the park. There was enough information from the news reports that I could piece things together in my head. We walked the trail of where she was last seen, and I started seeing things, small clues here and there."

He drained the last of his coffee and tossed the cup into a trashcan. "I had no idea if the cops had spotted them. I just took off, started following the signs."

"You left Cynthia on her own? Come on, man, you know better than that."

"I know, it just … it was like instinct or something. This urge to keep searching took over. Every unusual footprint or broken tree branch connected, even if they were far apart I could guess what way to go next." Nathan took a deep breath. "And I found her."

"Who?"

"The girl. Not her exactly, but I found where she'd been buried."

"Jesus, Nathan."

Recently turned soil at the base of a tree. The corner of a jacket sticking up through the earth. Two pale fingers under a leaf, the nail polish chipped. The memory forced its way into Nathan's vision.

"I ran. Nearly knocked Cynthia off her feet when she caught up to me. I didn't know what to do, or how to explain how I found her. Cynthia suggested we get to a payphone and call in an anonymous tip. So that's what we did. Ever since, we've been watching for unusual missing persons cases or animal attacks, finding out what we could and then sending tip-offs to the police. I don't know how I'm able to figure this stuff out."

"You always were good with small details."

Nathan blinked until the image of the park disappeared, bringing him back to the hospital. "You don't think I'm crazy?"

His friend wrapped an arm around his shoulder. "Who knows? I'm willing to hear you out. You're like a brother to me. I know you'd never make something like this up."

"Ben!" Laura had rounded the corner, holding a clipboard.

"How's Cynthia?" Ben asked.

Laura glanced over her clipboard. "Multiple minor lacerations to the face, hands, and elbows. Three broken ribs. Left forearm broken and left shoulder dislocated. Four fingers on the right hand broken, spiral fracture to the right wrist. Deep tissue bruising to both legs, stomach, and back. Fracture of the left femur. Minor bruising to the side of the skull and the throat."

She spoke with a trembling calm as she watched everyone's faces, trying to keep her tone neutral and professional.

Ben set back his shoulders and clenched his arm muscles. "Who did that to her?"

Laura shook her head. "It's hard to say. I mean, we think she was thrown around her office; we found small pieces of broken glass. Maybe a sledgehammer? I suppose if a couple of guys did it, if they were on PCP or something, they might have been able to cause that kind of damage on their own. But I can't figure why no one heard her screaming."

Nathan's mind flashed back to when he'd seen Eli, Gideon, and Creek in the medical examiner's office. The scene replayed in slow-motion in his mind. He recalled Roland's comments about seizing memories. Concentrating, Nathan watched the color fade from his memory, except for a bright patch of red on Eli's knuckles. The vampire had slipped his hands into his pockets as he winked at Nathan. The hands of the other two were clean.

"It was just one man." Nathan opened his eyes and saw the image of his memory fade back to the hospital. "One man did it, but he was with two others. And I know who he is."

"And you're going to the police, right?" Ben said.

Nathan shook his head. "No. The police can't do anything about this, but I know who can."

He turned to leave, but Ben caught hold of his arm. "You have to call the cops and tell them what you know. You can't go up against someone like that."

Nathan's face twisted. Did Ben think that little of him? Didn't Ben think he could take care of himself? His mind filled with an image of a snow-covered field. His shoulders felt heavy, tired from the weight of metal armor. Across from him was a figure he'd seen before, in his dreams. A man dressed like an ancient Roman soldier. Nathan's blood filled with rage and he swung his fist, scattering the image.

Ben caught his hand and bent the wrist back sharply. Nathan cried out in pain and dropped to his knees.

"What the hell?" Ben shouted.

Laura pulled on Ben's arm. "Let him up!"

He let go and stepped away. Nathan clutched his wrist. "I didn't mean … I'm sorry Nathan, I didn't think. What was that for?"

He couldn't tell them what he'd seen, what he'd felt. It was too much. "I'm sorry, Ben. I'm so sorry."

Nathan pulled himself to his feet. Laura stepped back and put her hand over her mouth. Her eyes glistened. Ben touched her shoulder, and she fell against him.

He felt ashamed, and scared. The emotion from that image had been so overpowering. He was just glad Ben had good reflexes. Firm grip, too. Small bruises were beginning to form where Ben's hand had clamped his fist.

Laura steadied her breathing and turned to Nathan. "I'm going to stay at Cynthia's place tonight." She held up her hand when Nathan began to protest. "She needs someone to look after her cat. I think it's for the best, just for now. Okay?"

Nathan nodded and sat down again.

"I have to get back to work," she said. "Ben, could you call Cynthia's sister in Philadelphia for me? Her family should know what happened."

"On it." He left to make some calls.

Laura stood over Nathan. "I'm going now."

"Yeah."

"You sticking with your story?"

"It's the truth."

"Right."

Laura turned sharply and walked away.

"Mind if I have a word, Mr. Shepherd?"

A leather-faced older man in a trench coat looked down at Nathan. He held a badge up in front of his stony face. Nathan gave a nod, and the man sat down next to him.

"I'm Detective Frank Powell. I'm sorry to hear about what happened to your friend."

"Excuse me?"

"Your girlfriend is Dr. Lucas? She told me you were the one who found Cynthia Keller in her office?"

"Oh. Yes, thank you."

"I'd like to ask you a few questions, if you don't mind?"

Nathan agreed, explaining again how he'd found Cynthia. This time he made up a story about them having arranged to meet for dinner, her not showing, and not answering her cell phone. The truth wouldn't be any help here.

"Your girlfriend didn't mention anything about that," Powell said. "But we only spoke briefly, just now."

Nathan searched for something to say. "She didn't know. We've been having problems."

"I see. So you and Dr. Keller were involved?"

"No, nothing like that. I was meeting her to get advice, you know?"

"Ah, of course." Powell took notes as he spoke. "Can you think of any reason why someone would want to hurt Dr. Keller?"

To get the information sitting on a flash drive in my pocket. "She's never hurt anyone in her life," Nathan said.

Powell took a small envelope from his coat pocket. He pulled out a photograph and handed it to Nathan. It was a fuzzy still taken from security camera footage. Three people standing in a doorway in a morgue. He recognized them immediately. It was Adams and the man and woman he worked with.

"This was taken around the time you found Dr. Keller," Powell said. "Moments before the camera shorted out. Do you recognize these people?"

"No."

Powell handed him another photograph. "We think they were looking at this woman's body," he said. "Her name is Miranda Grange. She was found about a week ago in an old building on the West Side. People matching the descriptions of these three individuals were seen in the area last night. One witness saw them entering the building through the roof. Looks like whoever killed Miss Grange was pretty unpleasant, doesn't it?"

Nathan said nothing.

"Mr. Shepherd, please, it's better if you cooperate. Are you certain you don't recognize these three people?"

"Am I under suspicion for anything here, Detective?"

"No, Mr. Shepherd," Powell said. "Not at all. I just thought you might be able to tell me something to help me find the people who hurt your friend, that's all."

"What about the security cameras near her office, Detective? What did they show?"

"Nothing. The cameras on that floor had a technical fault. Rather convenient, huh? You think about that picture, Mr. Shepherd. If you decide you know anything about what's happening, you give me a call."

Chapter Seven

"How long was I out?" Cynthia found it hard to hear her own voice, the words came out so soft.

"Just a couple of hours," Laura said. "I had to give you some morphine for the pain. We're going to do the surgery tomorrow, if that's okay?"

"Surgery?" Those men. Their faces taunted Cynthia in her mind.

"On your left leg. There's a break we'll need to pin back together." Laura looked out the window of the private room. Her lip quivered. With a long breath, she sat up straight and turned back to Cynthia. "Is it true? Did just one man do this?"

Cynthia blinked and did a quick review. The fingers on her right hand were splinted and bandaged. The cast around her left wrist and hand made it difficult to scratch that itch on her leg, which was suspended in a sling hanging from the bed frame. Her face felt swollen. At least the morphine kept the edge off the pain.

She nodded once, which was more than enough to make her dizzy. "There were three, but only one attacked me."

"There's a cop downstairs. You feel up to talking to him?"

Police. No, they would never buy into this. Vampire thugs beating a woman senseless for their supernatural gang boss? Not a chance.

"No."

"But he'll need descriptions so they can find these people."

"I'm not interested."

"Don't you want to press charges?"

"No. We'll handle this ourselves."

Laura got up from her chair. "You mean you and Nathan?"

"Yes."

"You don't believe that crap he's spouting, do you?"

"I've seen a lot of strange things lately. Things I can't explain in any purely scientific way. I have to keep an open mind."

Laura narrowed her eyes. "What exactly have you two been up to together?"

"What? Oh, come on, Laura. All we've been doing is hanging out and maybe checking out the news whenever some strange animal attack happens or someone goes missing."

"The two of you have been playing detective? What are you, twelve?"

"We help people."

"How?"

"We call in anonymous tips."

"If that's all, then why did someone attack you?"

"This time we found something different. Something dangerous and we're trying to stop it."

"Nathan dragged you into some gangland thing and you got hurt because of it?"

Cynthia jabbed two splinted fingers at Laura, making her back off. "I'm in this by my own choice. The only people responsible for what happened are the ones who barged into my office."

"But he asked you to get involved, right?"

"Yes."

"Why? He's talking about vampires and monsters. He's just playing some big game. He has to be. Why would you entertain this?"

"He's my friend. I trust him. Maybe you should give it a try, Laura. He loves you."

Laura gave a short laugh. "He never talks to me anymore. My best friend knows my boyfriend better than I do."

"There's nothing going on. Never was. We'd never do that to you."

Laura rubbed her forearms. "It's been a hard time. Sometimes I don't think he knows there's anything wrong."

"He can be a bit dense sometimes, huh?"

"Yeah." Laura's gaze fell to the floor.

"Next time you get some time alone, listen to him, okay? I know it's hard to believe some of the stuff he says, but he does love you, and if he could share his world with you, he would. It's not too late to fix things, right?"

"Right." Laura inhaled sharply and left the room.

At home Nathan dropped his keys into a small bowl on a table near the front door and hung up his jacket before dropping into an armchair. He sat, quietly going over the night's events while drumming his fingers. If this Creek character had taken Cynthia's flash drive, then they had important information, something which Adams and the others had broken into the morgue to find.

Nathan found himself shaking as he thought over what had happened. Delayed shock. He'd need something to keep his blood sugar levels steady. He made himself a cup of sweet tea while eating from a box of chocolate-covered raisins.

Sitting at his computer, he plugged in the flash drive and went to work.

Miranda's files were thorough. Nathan looked over the image files first. There were two large ones, both maps of Manhattan. One was a modern tourist map, while the other was a scan of an older map dating back to 1843. Much of the buildings from that time had long since been knocked down and built over. Other images were photographs of different places around New York. Some were of Eli and Gideon, always at night. She'd been following them.

There were scans of old history books, mostly relating to New York history. Nathan recognized the stamp of the New York Public Library on one of the images. There was a lot to get through. He got up to make some coffee.

Over the next few hours he went over the books Miranda had read, from accounts of certain families and businesses moving to New York long ago, to urban myths and legends from Europe and the Far East. She'd kept extensive notes. Nathan saw a pattern in the details she recorded.

Miranda had been investigating the deaths of the same people whose documents Murdoch and Sullivan had requested.

What was more, she'd found out what had killed them. All of them. Her notes were in a form of short-hand connecting the references to the myths and legends she'd researched.

A German word repeated itself, "Esser." It meant "eater." A piece of shorthand always preceded it, a rudimentary bird profile with a roughly human-shaped head. Nathan had seen something like it before. He glanced up to a shelf on the wall holding several books on ancient history. He took down one on ancient Egypt and flicked through the pages, quickly finding a matching symbol. *It's not shorthand.* It was a hieroglyph; the symbol for ba, the part of the soul ancient Egyptians believed made a person unique and lived on after death. Literally translated, Miranda was calling this thing "soul eater."

She didn't go into any detail about what the creature was or how it could be stopped. There was mention of an old section of the New York Public Library where she'd found the most accurate information. It contained volumes on a wide range of occult subjects. Nathan kept reading long into the early morning hours, finding out everything Miranda had done since coming to New York.

He felt the cold wind on his face. Nathan was a Roman soldier, a legate, a man of power and rank. Across from him was his general. A man he knew as Avitus, who had killed women and children. Enough was enough. Here in the snow, he would end it.

"You can't beat me, Lucius." Both men were tired from fighting. In each hand, they held a blade dripping with blood. The snow was streaked with red.

Nathan ran forward, attacking Avitus with all the strength left in him. The memory became blurred and confused. He tried to focus on it, as Roland had told him. Each attempt brought with it another stab of pain as Avitus struck him.

Eventually, the final blow came and Nathan fell to the ground. He watched Avitus walk away, leaving him to die in the snow.

The sound of the doorbell woke him. He'd fallen asleep at his computer. He had overslept, making him late for work. The doorbell rang again, urging Nathan to stand. He ached. The dream had left him with well-remembered sensations of ancient injuries. He limped to the front door.

It was Ben, who greeted him with a smile. Nathan invited him in and made some coffee. They sat in armchairs in the living room with the morning news on the television.

"Listen," Ben began. "Last night was kinda crazy, yeah? I mean, I'm sorry for what I did."

Nathan sipped his coffee. "I'm sorry, too. I didn't mean to try and hit you. Something just snapped, I guess." He shut his eyes. His wrist still hurt from the hold. "Did Laura tell you to come here?"

He shook his head. "No, she didn't." He leaned forward, running his hand through his hair. "I just don't want this, you know? Jesus, we're supposed to be friends. Look, I want to be supportive of this stuff you're into now, but I don't understand any of it."

"I'm seeing things from horror movies," Nathan said. "The more I learn, the more I want to look away, but I can't. It's like I'm drawn to it. You wouldn't believe the things I know."

Ben looked up. "Try me."

Nathan shook his head. "Not after what happened to Cynthia. You guys are safer if you don't know anything."

"I can handle myself."

"I can tell." He rubbed his wrist. "You're like a bear."

"Well, you did try to hit me. That's not normal behavior, is it?" Ben glanced at the news. There was a report of a dead body found close to Broadway.

"It's not a normal world, Ben." Nathan watched the news story. The victim's name hadn't been released, but the location was close enough to the other murder sites that it gave him some concern. "I'm going through some strange things right now. Seeing things that aren't real, like when someone remembers something upsetting from the past and all the emotion comes back, except this is a hundred times worse. Like I'm living it again. I can't explain it without making myself sound crazy."

He nodded. "Just promise me you're going to be careful, okay?"

"You got it."

"You can talk to me. I'm your friend. You need anything, I'm here, got it?"

Ben left, and Nathan headed out soon after. He'd left his sports bag on the passenger seat of his car. Making sure he had fresh batteries for his flashlight, he also packed a couple of bottles of water and some granola bars.

This drive proved to be very different from previous journeys into the city. Nathan was acutely aware now of people who looked just a little out of place. He began wondering if every crazed-looking bum was a secret wizard or a werewolf. He made guesses at those who were 'in the trade' as Roland had put it.

The guesses developed into an instinctive sense for who might be involved in the world of the supernatural. He was becoming aware of an overlooked subculture that was as much a part of the city as the stockbrokers and Broadway wannabes.

Nathan found parking near the New York Public Library and fed the meter with enough quarters to last until afternoon. Finding the section Miranda had described was fairly easy. It was tucked away with its own little reading room. The archway into the section had a simple plaque reading only *Older Texts*, but an inscription on the marble of the arch read *Memento Mori*. Nathan recognized it as an old Latin saying that meant 'remember you must die.' A reminder that even the most powerful people have to die and face judgment.

Miranda's notes mentioned a Thaddeus Morningway, a powerful wizard connected to the soul eater. The books here were not listed on the library's computer, making it difficult to locate a specific text.

He turned to the others in the room. "Um," he began. "Can anyone tell me where to find a book about Thaddeus Morningway?"

The people shrugged.

"He was eh … a wizard? Came here in about 1804?" Despite everything, Nathan still felt a little foolish to be asking such a question.

A bearded man in the corner spoke up. "Ah, you want *19th Century Witches and Warlocks of the East Coast.* Here." The man approached the shelves and plucked a book. "Enjoy. And good luck, young man."

"Thank you … I think."

The old man smiled and returned to his seat. Nathan sat with the book and opened the cracked leather cover.

Thaddeus Morningway had spent some time in Boston before coming to New York. Details about his early life were sketchy, but he was a known dabbler in alchemy and was suspected in the abduction of three young men in 1806. Most of his work had been into trying to determine the fate of the human soul after passing on, and he had conducted many experiments to cross the barrier between life and death. He blackmailed, bought, coerced, and drugged people to use them as subjects in his work.

Later in his life, Morningway had started to gain a reputation as a summoner of spirits and demons, and some believed he sold his soul for the power to control such creatures.

Nathan stopped on an old photograph of Morningway. It had been among a collection assembled as an accessory to the book he was reading. He was dressed as a gentleman of the time, with a fine suit and a top hat. He had deep-set eyes and a hawkish nose, with wispy mutton chop sideburns.

Next to him in the picture was his wife, Elisabeth. She looked young enough to be his granddaughter. Long dark hair, pale skin, a gentle smile. She was beautiful. Around her neck she wore a dragonfly pendant, and her dress was decorated with such fine embroidery that the full detail was lost in the old photograph. Something about her eyes told Nathan he'd seen her before, but he couldn't place where.

He found little mention of Elisabeth Morningway anywhere. It was interesting that a man obsessed with death would marry someone so young. Perhaps he had viewed her as a kind of respite. Something to remind him that, despite his research, he was still alive. Something to cherish. Nathan could understand the need for that. Thoughts of Laura found their way into his mind, but he pushed them aside.

Toward the end of Morningway's life he had begun to experiment with actually mastering control over the dead. He branched from demon summoning into necromancy, binding a number of ghosts to his service. Nathan sat back in his chair and closed the book.

Morningway and his wife died in a fire shortly before the very first deaths on the list that Murdoch and Sullivan had sent into his office. It was possible that Morningway had summoned the soul eater. Perhaps it had even been responsible for his death?

Now that he had a theory as to what had started the killings, Nathan needed to find out what a soul eater was and see if the pieces fit.

"Does anyone know where I can find information on soul eaters?"

All eyes rose and fixed on him. The same bearded patron who had shown him the book leaned across his table and whispered, "Best not to ask those kinds of questions. Look into the abyss, sure, but nothing good comes of prodding it with a stick."

Nathan left the library and took out his cell phone. He called Roland. "I need to know everything about soul eaters."

There was silence for a while. "Roland? You there?"

"I'm here." There was a tremor in his voice. "Nathan, where did you hear that term?"

"Miranda Grange's notes. She was on to something. I think a soul eater is responsible for all these deaths. What can you tell me?"

"Nothing you'll like, and nothing I'd like to say over the phone. You told Adams yet?"

"No."

"Tell him," Roland replied. "He needs to know how dangerous the situation is. He should know where my place is. If he wants, he can meet us there, tonight."

Nathan reached his car. "Sure, no problem. Roland, how bad could this be?"

"Lemme put it this way, kid," Roland said. "They don't call them soul eaters because they make daisy chains and dance in meadows."

Roland hung up. It was frustrating enough that no one else had given Nathan a straight answer on anything, but this soul eater business was worse.

Adams would have to listen now. Nathan had valuable information and if Adams's team was only expecting vampires, they would need all the information they could get.

Nathan held his breath as he dialed. Adams's number rang out three times before he finally answered.

"For the last time, Shepherd, stay out of this."

"I know what killed Miranda Grange."

Adams was silent for a while. Nathan heard talking in the background.

"Go on," Adams said.

"I have copies of her notes, the ones you've been looking for. I'll share everything, but I want in on this. I can help."

"How did you know? You know what, never mind. Who killed Miranda?"

"It was a soul eater."

"A soul eater." Someone swore in the background. "Are you certain?" Adams sounded nervous, and he spoke too quickly for Nathan to respond. "Nathan, are you certain?"

"Yes. I worked out Miranda's shorthand."

"I figured she was hunting some kind of predator, but I didn't think it was this. It explains some things, all right. Do you have anywhere safe we can meet?"

"Roland's place in Riverside Park."

"Roland's still around? Sure, that'll do. Nine o'clock tonight."

"So I'm in?"

"I didn't say that. Just meet us at Roland's tonight. We'll see where to go from there."

"All right, but—"

Adams hung up. Nathan swore quietly and drove off. His first stop was to a sporting goods store where he bought himself a wooden baseball bat. The store had a section for camping and outdoor survival gear, so he also picked up a camping knife, a small flare gun, and a pack of six flares.

He then stopped off at a convenience store selling small bottles of holy water. He bought a dozen bottles.

A man in a grey suit walked up to him as he left the store, flanked by two other, larger men wearing leather jackets. Subtle bulges sat underneath their left arms. Handguns in shoulder holsters.

"Mr. Shepherd?" Nathan had seen this man before, at the medical examiner's office. "I'm Jonah Creek. I work for a man you need to meet."

A black limo pulled up and Creek opened the door. "My employer is a busy man, and his hospitality is not rejected lightly. You may leave your groceries in your car."

Nathan tossed the shopping bag into his car and got into the limo. He sat back, with the two thugs pressing on either side of him. Creek sat across from him.

"Drink?"

Nathan shook his head.

"Relax, Mr. Shepherd. You seem tense."

"Sure, I'm used to relaxing when two Neanderthals packing heat squash me into a limo while my car wracks up more parking tickets."

"My employer will take care of your car. Are you sure you wouldn't like a drink?"

"I'm fine, thanks."

Nathan watched the buildings pass by, noting where he was being taken. The silence was uncomfortable but no more than trying to make conversation with Creek.

The limo pulled up outside a tall office building. The thugs got out and left the door open for Nathan. He climbed out and looked up at the building. He knew the address.

He walked forward ahead of Creek and stepped into the lobby of Murdoch and Sullivan's corporate headquarters.

Chapter Eight

THE ELEVATOR SHAFT WAS BUILT UP ALONG THE corner of the building, so those inside could see out and watch the city fall lower below them as they rose. It was an ancient mind strategy. Rulers would often build the roads to their cities, castles, and palaces in such a way that a traveler would be exposed to the most imposing views for the longest time possible. It was intended to both impress and intimidate, making sure anyone coming to them would be suitably informed of the king's greatness.

The elevator stopped and Creek led Nathan down a corridor with floor to ceiling windows looking out at the city. Paintings by famous artists from all over the world lined the other wall. The two goons followed like trained dogs.

It took all Nathan's effort to keep his hands from shaking. They reached a set of heavy, ebony doors at the end of the corridor, only faintly distinguishable from the wall. Creek pressed his hand against part of the wall and the doors opened to reveal another elevator. This one was also built with glass, looking out at the city. There were only two buttons set into an ornate brass panel. Creek pressed the button to go up.

When the doors opened again, Nathan looked down a long corridor with no windows, just black walls stretching away from him. The floor was tiled with stone slabs with lights set into the floor. Gold-framed paintings of depictions from *Dante's Inferno* were spaced out at regular intervals.

"Go on, Mr. Shepherd." Creek stayed in the elevator with the two goons while Nathan stepped into the hall.

Where the building lobby and previous halls had been bright, spacious, and airy, this was dark and claustrophobic. Nathan felt the black walls crushing down on him, almost seeing writhing shapes move behind the sheen of the marble. He reached the end of the corridor and another barely-visible door opened up.

The office was a stark contrast to the hall. It was wide and open, with light streaming in from a wall of windows. Luxurious upholstered couches sat around wide, marble coffee tables set into slightly sunken pits. A long, grey meeting table stood between the couches and a broad desk at the end of the room. A leather office chair sat behind it, turned to face away from Nathan.

"Welcome, Mr. Shepherd." The voice was like churning gravel.

"Thanks," he said, walking toward the desk. "Dorian, I presume?" He tried to keep his breathing steady.

The chair spun slowly and Nathan found himself meeting an angular face which swooped down like a bird of prey, framed by long black hair. Pale grey eyes, white teeth splitting a thin smile. The nod of Dorian's head struck Nathan like a hammer.

"Figured that out, did you?"

"The vampires Eli and Gideon work for you. They and Mr. Creek back there are responsible for the attack on my friend last night. They say you run things around here. It makes sense you'd be in charge of one of the biggest companies in the city."

"Very clever."

"Are you Murdoch or Sullivan?"

"Neither. They work for me. This is a legitimate company carrying out legitimate business. I only happen to own all the shares, one way or another. Please, sit."

"I'd rather not."

Dorian's eyes darkened, though his smile never faltered. "Then perhaps a drink?"

A woman appeared from a back room. Long alabaster legs and pin-up model blonde hair. Her business suit accentuated her curves as she moved. "What can I get for you both?"

"I'm driving," Nathan said.

She sauntered over to a bar close to a bank of flat-screen televisions where she poured a glass of whiskey, neat. She brought the drink to Dorian and left quietly.

"Thank you, Persephone," Dorian said. "It's important to have good help. Now then, back to business."

He stood and circled the table to look out through the windows. Something about him was familiar. Nathan's mind began to wander.

He pictured a dinner party. Everyone was dressed in fine clothes, 19th century, maybe. A sea of faces parted and Nathan saw Dorian look back at him, his hair shorter and tidier, wearing a ruffled shirt under a dinner jacket. Nathan crossed the room with dream-like fluidity. He was shorter than Dorian. Vulnerability quickly evolved into fear, then hatred. The experience was fleeting, but enough to make him wary.

"You don't work for Adams," Dorian said. "I'm guessing you're presently unaffiliated with the rest of the reborn."

"I work alone."

He smirked. "We both know that isn't true. Ms. Keller carried out some work for you, you've got a friend following you around the city, and then of course there's Roland."

"Roland has only answered my questions. I understood that was within the rules."

"It is, of course. Merely an observation."

"You mentioned someone following me?"

"Not a friend? Better watch your step, then, Mr. Shepherd. You're drawing more and more attention every day. You should look over your shoulder once in a while."

Dorian was trying to distract him. "You requested those documents from the Department of Records," Nathan said. "The deaths happening in ten-year cycles. I processed the request myself."

"I can't take credit for that. I believe you've heard of Miranda Grange?"

Nathan's breath caught in his throat.

"She began working here as an office clerk some months ago. I learned that she forged signatures on some official documents and looked into it. She was the one who made the request. I had my people keep an eye on her. Because I wanted to learn what she was doing, I contacted your office and made sure I got the documents."

"Do you ignore all cases of fraud committed by your employees?"

"In my particular line of business it pays to learn as much as possible about any inconsistency before taking rash action." Dorian sipped his drink.

"I know about the soul eater." The words came too fast and too desperate.

Dorian set his glass down and traced a finger around the rim.

"Cynthia was able to tell me, before she was brought to the hospital," Nathan lied. He didn't want Dorian knowing about Cynthia's flash drive.

"What did she tell you?"

"Just the name." Nathan chewed on the inside of his lip.

Dorian narrowed his eyes. "It's infuriating, isn't it? That need to know. The drive to learn, to discover. It seems we're quite alike."

"I'm nothing like you."

Dorian flashed perfect teeth. "You won't learn anything about the soul eater in a library." He drained his glass and went to the bar to pour another. "I'm sure I can offer you some answers."

Without asking, he poured a glass for Nathan and came back with it. Nathan accepted it out of politeness.

"Of course," Dorian went on, "such information is valuable, and there would be a price."

Nathan sniffed the scotch. His dad would have loved it. "My soul?"

Dorian laughed. "Don't be so dramatic. No, Mr. Shepherd, I want you to work for me."

"What?"

"You're young, eager, and you seem to have a gift for investigation. Odds are, if you continue on your own, you will either get yourself killed or end up working for me anyway. Why not skip the middle ground?"

"And what if I end up working against you?"

"See the first option, Mr. Shepherd."

"There have to be other people in this city who would stand up against you."

"Maybe once. But they're long gone."

"What about Robert Adams?" Nathan hoped he wasn't tipping his hand, but he wanted to see if he could rattle Dorian, even a little.

"Adams is an irritation. And he has no honor." Dorian sat back down at his desk. "Don't kid yourself, Mr. Shepherd. The last thing the people of this city want is another so-called hero to get their hopes up and then abandon them when things get rough."

"He wouldn't." Dorian had to be lying. There had to be *someone* who cared about the city. If Adams wasn't going to help, and Roland couldn't, who else was there?

"What has he done to prove otherwise? The man is a killer and a coward. Me? I bring order and stability. Where there was chaos and pain I brought security. You don't know the suffering that this city felt before the war. Before me, Adams and his kind let all manner of abominations run free. It was anarchy bred of the notion that everyone: mundane, wizard, reborn, vampire, werewolf, demon, all had their own equal rights. I changed that."

"Your men hurt Cynthia. You call that order?"

"I'm sorry for that. But if you agree to work for me, you'll have standing in our world, and we can address your grievance in the correct manner. You must understand the need for rules and due process?"

"Unless someone works for you, they don't matter?"

"No, Mr. Shepherd. Unless they work for me, I can't protect them. Rules are rules."

"Right." Nathan stood and stepped back. "I think we're done here."

"As you wish." Dorian motioned with his hand toward the elevator. "The offer stands. Think it over."

"I won't need to." He stopped for a moment, and then turned to face Dorian. "I think we have met before. I knew you in another life."

Nathan forced himself to meet the man's cold grey eyes. "We were enemies."

Dorian inhaled deeply. "In that case may I point out that I'm still alive?" He let a small silence hang in the air. "This means, if we were in fact enemies, that you have never defeated me."

Nathan was the one who had died and been born again. Dorian was still alive. As was Eli. Images of both of them, grinning in victory, swam in Nathan's memories, his fear too great to concentrate on sorting through them. As he reached the elevator, he prayed Creek wouldn't notice his hands trembling.

Nathan was escorted out of the building and returned to his car. He found that the parking meter had been kept paid up in his absence, as promised. He thought about what Dorian had said, about someone following him. He hadn't noticed anyone tailing him. He tried to remember something suspicious during the day.

He found the effort frustratingly difficult. Though his mind's eye swam with images, he couldn't pick out what he was looking for. Remembering the blood on Eli's hands had been easy. He had a single memory and image on which to focus his thoughts. Trying to remember if he'd seen one specific car or person in the flood of New York traffic was a daunting task, and one which he really didn't have time to tackle while the parking meter was slowly ticking away.

Nathan got back into his car and resolved to keep a sharper eye out. He could call Ben or Laura, bring them along to the meeting with Adams. Ben seemed like he wanted to help, and maybe it would help convince Laura that he wasn't crazy or making it all up. *But what if they end up like Cynthia?* Maybe it was best not to bring them.

Besides, Adams seemed determined to want Nathan kept at arm's length. If he showed up with other people, Adams might shut him out completely.

It was while he'd stopped to pick up something to eat that Nathan spotted the silver saloon. He hadn't seen it until he'd gotten back to his car with a meatball sandwich and a Coke, but he recognized it immediately as Ben's car.

He pulled out into traffic, keeping an eye on his rear-view mirror. Ben stayed only a few cars behind. Nathan drove to Riverside Park and called Ben's cell phone.

"Pull over," he instructed.

He watched Ben pull into a parking spot several yards back. Nathan got out and walked over. Ben rolled down his window.

"What do you think you're doing?" Nathan asked him.

"I want to help get the guys who beat up Cynthia. I know that's what you're doing, and I want to help you."

"You don't want to get involved in this," Nathan said.

"I saw those guys take you away in the car," Ben said, "and those people in the library when you were there. I believe you, Nathan. I believe the things you've seen. I can help."

"This is dangerous. I've been attacked twice. Sooner or later, I'm going to run out of luck, and if that happens when a friend of mine is there..." He shook his head. "I want to get information to the people who can make a difference. I want to help them stop this killer."

"And after that?"

Nathan shook his head. "I don't know. I'm falling into something bigger than anything I could have imagined. I'm scared, Ben. Right now I'll be happy to keep making it day by day. After it's over, I still have to sort things out with Laura."

"Have the family life, like she wants?"

"Yeah. I mean, I want it to, it's just..."

"What?"

"It's hard to see how things can be normal again after this."

"Well, you're going to have to."

Nathan frowned. "What?"

"How long have you been putting her on hold? Was it five years ago she first started talking about marriage?"

Five years, six months, and three days. The dates skipped through his thoughts. They had been out for an anniversary dinner.

"I've been—"

"Stop." Ben clenched his fist and shook it at Nathan. Don't even start with the excuses, I've heard them all. Whatever else is going on, you're dragging Laura along. Man up and give her what she wants, or let her go so she can find someone who will. You got me?"

Nathan's wrist twinged where Ben had bent it back in the hospital. "It's not that simple."

"Make it that simple."

"Look, I can't worry about it right now. I'm meeting some people tonight. I've got information for them. I have to finish this."

Ben leaned on the steering wheel. "These friends of yours. They're going to put a stop to whatever's going on?"

"I hope so."

"And you want to help them find out how to do it?"

"Yeah."

He exhaled slowly, focusing his eyes somewhere in the distance. "Then I'm helping you."

"Damn it, Ben."

"I want in on this. Cynthia thought this was important enough to help. I can't call myself your friend if I don't make damn sure you follow through, the right way. If you try to ditch me, I swear to you, Nathan, I will tell the cops everything for your own good, got it?"

Nathan believed him. "All right," he sighed. "You're in. But I can't let these other people know about you. They're already having enough trouble trusting me. I can't figure out my next move until I've spoken to them. You have my word I'll fill you in on everything tomorrow, and before I do anything dangerous, okay?"

"Okay, deal." He started his car and pulled away.

Nathan walked through the park and watched the sun set across the harbor. At last it was time to go to Roland's.

He was the first to arrive at nine o'clock. Roland welcomed him inside with a hot mug of coffee. It wasn't long before Adams arrived and everyone crowded into the living room. Roland hovered near the kitchen in case his guests needed anything. Every one of them had claimed the right of sanctuary upon entering, under Adams's insistence.

Nathan sat on a stool near the fireplace, hunched over his coffee. The stern, burly man and caramel-skinned woman with Adams, who introduced themselves as Jim Lane and Cadence Brooke, shared a two-seater couch while Adams sat back in an armchair.

They listened while Nathan told them about everything that had happened, right up to and including his meeting with Dorian, but he lied about Ben, instead telling them he'd kept his friend out of this.

"You did the right thing," Adams said. "Both in refusing to deal with Dorian and making sure your friend stayed out of harm's way."

"I don't understand," Nathan said. "If this soul eater has been waking to feed every ten years, why are you and Dorian only looking for it now?"

"It's not that simple, Nathan," Cadence said. "New York has always been a hotly contested territory." She sat back with one leg lying across the other. "Factions have had their representatives here, each vying for power. Then the war happened." She turned to Lane, as if handing the story over to him.

"Leaders decided to fight," Lane continued. "A lot of people died. We lost."

Cadence's face fell into a frown. Lane glanced at her and shrugged.

"Tensions heated up," she said. "Eventually everyone took sides or got the hell out of Dodge. The vampires, necromancers, even some shape shifters and regular wizards, all sided with the Council of Chains. Meanwhile, any mundane humans in the trade willing to fight, the majority of the sane witches and wizards, and some local spirits, sided with the Conclave."

"What's the Conclave?" Nathan asked.

"It's sort of a union of those in the trade who seek mutual protection and help. There've been Conclaves in every major populated area for as long as there've been people walking the planet. Mostly they're made up of reborn warriors, scholars, and wizards. But they accept anyone who hasn't violated the Second of the Common Laws."

That sparked something in Nathan's mind, but he let Cadence continue.

"The Common Laws are generally accepted guidelines on what is and is not considered morally and ethically right. The First Law instructs us to live free, but bring no harm to others. The Second Law is that the cycle of life and death is sacred and unending. Any attempt to corrupt, defy, or undo the cycle is forbidden."

"You mean like how the Council works."

"Exactly. They've been around since the height of the Roman Empire, preying on peoples' fears about what happens to us between the moment we die and the time we're reincarnated. They gained enough support to ignore some of the Common Laws, but their members can become dangerous because of how many of them need to prey on humans to survive. Wars between the Council and local Conclaves have happened throughout history. The one for the East Coast was the most recent."

"We lost," Lane added.

Adams nodded. "New York was one of the territories we had to surrender outright. Boston remains ours, while Philadelphia belongs to them. D.C.'s neutral ground for the time being."

"What does all this have to do with the soul eater?" Nathan asked. "Why haven't these killings gotten anyone's attention before?"

"Until now, there hasn't been one single ruler of the city," Cadence said. "Most areas of the world are inhabited by a number of factions struggling back and forth for power. But when the East Coast War ended, Dorian became the first to have sole control of an entire populated area in over a thousand years. Now he controls the police and city government. He has influence on the state level. Quite frankly, he's a mastermind, a tactical and political genius with almost two hundred years of experience in his current incarnation alone."

"Now Dorian can spare the resources to find this thing," Cadence went on. "If he does, and works out how to control it, he'll have a nearly unstoppable weapon."

Roland brought in a fresh round of coffee then went back to the kitchen door where he lit up a cigarette. Nathan noticed his hands were shaking.

"Everyone would fear him," Cadence said. "Soul eaters are the most feared and despised predators in the world. Their victims are trapped. Locked inside the soul eater. They can never pass on to the next life. Soul eaters are bestial. They lie dormant for years at a time, waking regularly to feed."

"And now it's back and it got Miranda." Lane said, staring into his mug.

"Why did she come here in the first place?" Nathan asked. "According to her notes, she didn't know she was chasing a soul eater from the start."

"Twenty years ago," Cadence explained, "Miranda lost her parents. She was young then, only beginning to grasp her new memories. Then the war began and there was no time to investigate. When we were forced to leave New

York and retreat to Boston several years later, she was heartbroken. Ten years ago, when the soul eater would likely have woken last, she spotted connections in reports of mysterious deaths, just like you did. She found out the bodies looked the same as her parents' when they were found. She did what work she could from Boston, learning about the past murders. A few months ago, in violation of the East Coast Treaty, she came here to pre-empt the next wave and find out what was causing them."

"Where does that leave us?" Nathan asked.

"The three of us won't be enough to hunt the soul eater," Adams said. "I've contacted some friends back in Boston and sent for help. I've also been in touch with Council representatives in D.C. to seek permission for the hunt."

"You mean you're not supposed to be here?"

"Entering Dorian's territory to bring back one of our own who entered without permission is a minor transgression," Adams said. "The Council would view it more like cleaning up our own mess. But if a lot of armed outsiders show up, it could be seen as an attack, which would cause trouble for our allies in D.C. and possibly end in an assault on Boston."

"Which, quite frankly, we're not in a position to defend against," Cadence said.

Adams shot her a glare. "Hopefully, Dorian will choose to save face. He'll allow us to enter and, publicly at least, assist us in the hunt."

"And in reality?" Nathan scratched at the table's surface.

"He'll send agents against us and swear he knew nothing about it," Adams replied. "He might sacrifice a patsy to keep things friendly, too. Make no mistake, Dorian wants that thing, and if we do receive any help from him, it'll be so he can use us to find it for him before he stabs us all in the back."

"What next?"

"Recon," Lane said. "Find its nest; watch in case it tries to feed."

"I'm in."

"No." Adams stood and pulled on his long coat. "You're not. Cadence will go to your place with you to get the flash drive. Then you'll bring her back here. You've got potential, but you're not ready to fight a soul eater."

Chapter Nine

"We don't need the flash drive," Nathan said. "I've gone over everything on it, and I remember it. I'm good at that."

They'd spent most of the drive in silence, Nathan trying to work up the courage to talk and try to convince Cadence he could help.

"Eidetic memory?" She perked up her eyebrows up. "Some reborn are able to extend their ability to recall memories into their present incarnation. It's a useful gift. But unfortunately, it doesn't do the rest of us much good for helping in the research."

"Tell me about this East Coast Treaty. Technically, none of you guys are allowed to be here?" Nathan asked.

"All reborn who fought against the Council in the war, like Adams and Lane, were banished from New York, along with their immediate families. Any reborn from outside New York were likewise forbidden to enter the city without permission. The treaty was signed on the winter solstice under a binding ritual to make sure any Conclave-allied spirits couldn't break it. Mortals can, of course, but it's dangerous for us to come here."

"What are the odds of anyone coming rushing to take Dorian?"

"Non-existent. Sorry."

Nathan clenched the steering wheel. "What about me, now? Do I have to leave too?"

Cadence smiled, her thin face pretty in the dim light. "You're different. You didn't fight in the war, so you're exempt from the treaty. You can do as you like."

"Then shouldn't Adams be asking for my help?"

"He's a good field leader," Cadence said, leaning back against the headrest. "But he's set in his ways. Lane's been with him since the war. I was just a kid when they arrived in Boston, but my mother was a well-known witch and helped them out. I've worked with him on a few different things. Mostly exorcisms or banishings. You're new, and you're untested. But he'll warm to you."

"What's so special about New York, anyway?"

Cadence stared out the window. "It's all politics and history. The same way one soul can be known for certain things and become more adept at them, places can be known for things. Their energy is attuned to certain ways of life. When most parts of the American supernatural underworld were closing up their borders and keeping out newcomers, New York kept taking people in, regardless of where they came from, similar to how it was with mundane immigrants. A place like that can then become so prominent in the minds of people that the very idea of the place has its own power. Even without the ancient rites and spells used in the city's design, and believe me, there were a lot. The fact is that New York is a vast reservoir of emotional power. That energy can be tapped to fuel large-scale magic. Few cities so young have such power."

"And Dorian controls that power."

"Yeah, and with the treaty backing him, he can use that power whenever he wants."

Nathan pulled into his driveway. The lights were off. He led Cadence to the house. "Can you banish the soul eater?"

"Never fought one before. Most predators like this are creatures from another dimension, and it's definitely an option. If we kill it, the souls it consumed will be freed, and they can pass on at last. Killing the soul eater might be harder than sending it back to its own realm, but we have to try."

"How do we kill it?"

"Soul eaters are astral beings. They have no solid form of their own and only strike when their prey is weak. They can be destroyed when they manifest, although it's not easy. For them to take on a permanent physical form, which it would have to in order to cause the slash marks you found, it needs to be ritually bound into a physical body, typically a fresh corpse. They carry a phylactery, an enchanted talisman like a crystal or glass jar, which houses their essence. If you destroy it, the soul eater dies."

"Sounds easy enough," Nathan said, smirking.

Cadence frowned. "Yeah, which is why no one's managed it in a hundred and fifty years."

They went inside and Nathan got the flash drive from a small safe in the wall. It was where he kept valuables like his mother's wedding ring and important documents such as the deed to the house. He handed the flash drive to Cadence, who stared at the small lump of plastic.

"Miranda was a good friend," Cadence said. "This is the last bit of her we have left. Until we kill the soul eater." She reached up and kissed Nathan on the cheek. "Thank you for keeping this safe."

Nathan smiled and opened his mouth to speak, but stopped when he looked past Cadence to see Laura standing in the doorway.

Shit.

Laura's face flashed with anger. "Who is this?"

Cadence turned quickly. "Oh, hi." She reached out, offering to shake Laura's hand. "I'm Cadence. Your husband is helping us—"

"We're not married," Laura said. She walked past Cadence and stopped inches from Nathan. "What's going on here?"

Nathan went to speak, but Laura cut him off before he got a word out. "Have you been going behind my back with this tramp? My God, I thought you'd be more man than that. Did Cynthia know? Was she covering for you? Is that what was going on?"

Nathan was growing tired of this. He didn't expect Laura to believe in any of the things he'd learned, but he'd never been unfaithful to her. Yet here she was, jumping at the chance to have it out with him. Again.

"I don't have time to explain, but I'm not having an affair. We're going now. I'm not sure when I'll be home." He walked around Laura and started for the door.

"You get out," Laura said to Cadence. "Get out of my house." She pulled her hand back and swung at the girl's face. Nathan moved to get between them, too slowly, as Cadence caught Laura's arm at the wrist and twisted it, using the momentum to spin Laura and push her up against the wall.

"I'm not getting involved in whatever's going on between you two," Cadence said. "But I've killed vampires, hunted werewolves, and undone the magic of demons. You raise a hand to me again and I will break it." She released the hold and Laura cradled her arm. "I suggest you get your temper under control, or it could land you in a lot of trouble."

Nathan offered an apologetic glance to Laura as Cadence walked outside. "I'm sorry. I'll…"

"Just go," she replied in a jagged voice.

Nathan followed Cadence back to the car. "Was that really necessary?"

"Sorry." She clipped her seatbelt shut. "I was in an abusive relationship in a past life. More than one, actually. Left its mark. I react badly to people hitting me."

Only a week ago, Nathan would have found that explanation to be insane. Tonight he couldn't think of a better reason for her behavior. He started the car.

"Those marks on her arms." Cadence broke the silence somewhere close to the bridge. "Those are bruises caused by someone grabbing her."

"I've never raised a hand to Laura in my life."

"Your hands aren't quite big enough to cause marks that size."

"I think it happened at work," Nathan said. "She's a doctor in an ER. We don't talk much these days."

"If Laura hasn't had the dreams remembering past lives, if she doesn't believe the things you're telling her are real, it'll just get harder for you both."

"When the soul eater is dead, I'm done. I want my old life back," Nathan said.

"It might be harder than you think."

"Why?" he asked.

"Our research suggests that the more a particular soul lives certain kinds of lifestyles, the more likely that person is to follow the same path in future incarnations. We get better at our old skills. Take me, for example. I've been a wizard or a witch over and over again, so it comes naturally to me. Same as what happened with your girlfriend back there. Each part of a lifetime has an impact on the next."

"Even death?"

"Especially death. A painful or traumatic death can delay a reincarnation, making it harder to reunite with people you once knew. It can leave deep emotional scars that take lifetimes to heal."

"Are you saying that I'm destined to live the same kind of lives I've had before?"

"Not quite. But if you used to be a warrior, then that's what you're going to be best at. All that skill and knowledge is locked away, waiting to be released. It's literally what you were born to do."

"Maybe. But what if Adams is right and I'm not cut out for this? If I haven't had time to get good enough? I want Laura. I want a good job, kids. A family. That's what I've always wanted."

"Does Laura know that?"

Nathan didn't reply. He realized his silence said enough, and he slumped in the seat.

"Let me ask you this, then," Cadence said. "Why are you getting involved at all if you want a normal life?"

"They went after Cynthia because she was helping me. I can't let that lie. I won't bail now."

"But once the soul eater's dead, you're done."

"Exactly."

She laughed softly. "I said that myself once."

Nathan kept his eyes on the road. What did Cadence know about him anyway?

It was after midnight when they re-grouped with Adams and Lane at Roland's place. Nathan sat by the fireplace, a hot coffee the only thing standing between him and exhausted sleep. Adams had spent a while looking over Miranda's notes on a laptop while Lane had circled locations on a street map using a permanent marker, adding in extra marks for recent deaths reported in the news which could be attributed to the soul eater.

"We don't have the manpower for a complete sweep of its hunting grounds," Adams said.

"I'm not talking about a complete sweep," Lane said. "Key locations, start at the murder spot, spread out and look for signs of the thing. It's just an animal. We stand a much better chance of finding it if we stick to its hunting pattern as much as possible."

"Fine." Adams shook his head and leafed through the notes some more. "Most of its activity has been concentrated on these districts."

He picked up a red felt pen and circled several areas between Riverside Park and Hell's Kitchen.

"Right. These are the places it's killed so far." Lane jabbed his pen down on the locations of this year's victims. "And there are places from when it woke in previous years to feed that we should keep an eye on."

"Agreed."

Nathan stared into his coffee. They weren't thinking things through. The soul eater didn't just kill and move on to another area for its next victim.

"What about when you tracked it to where it killed Miranda?" he asked. "It killed another person near the same building."

"Miranda most likely stumbled on it." Adams glanced at Lane briefly. "She wasn't its intended target."

"But that shows the soul eater doesn't always leave a place alone after killing there."

Lane reached over and placed a hand on Nathan's shoulder. "I know. But the odds say that we're more likely to run into it if we stick to the areas where it hasn't killed yet."

"And if it decides to kill someone somewhere you're not looking?"

Lane shook his head a little.

"Acceptable risk," Adams said. "We can't be everywhere at once."

That wasn't good enough. "There's got to be some way to find it without waiting for it to kill again," Nathan said.

"If you've got some brilliant plan for tracking it down, Shepherd, I'm listening." Nathan said nothing. "No? Okay, then."

"We should wait for daylight," Lane said.

Adams rubbed his chin. "I'm not sure I like giving Dorian's people time to move on this. I don't think he'll pass up a chance to make a play for the soul eater."

"His vampires won't be active during the day, though."

"He'll have other agents on the streets."

"It's still one less thing to worry about."

"I don't care— "

"Pack it in, boys," Cadence said. "There's nothing in Miranda's notes about controlling the soul eater. So even if there is a way, Dorian's going to need time to figure out how to do it. That gives us some time to rest up and get ready."

"Fine," Adams said. "Daylight it is. Lane, Cadence, we'll start here tomorrow, 8 am." He pressed his finger down on the site of one of the murders, near DeWitt Clinton Park.

"Let me come," Nathan said.

"Not a chance," he shot back.

"Between Miranda, and other similar deaths in the soul eater's hunting ground, I count seven deaths. It'll probably only kill another three or so before going back into hibernation, assuming it sticks to its previous behavior. You're going to need all the help you can get." Nathan felt Roland and Cadence's eyes on him.

"You've obviously got your ears to the ground in this city," Adams said. "You hear of anything we might need to know, call me. But stay off the streets."

"I can help," Nathan insisted.

"Not by getting yourself killed." Adams walked out of the room with Lane close behind him. Cadence gave Nathan's arm a squeeze as she passed him, but just shook her head when he went to speak.

"It's amazing," Roland said after they had left. "How often someone like Adams asks to use my place as a safe haven to make their plans, and never once thinks to ask if I know anything that could help, me being a completely neutral party, and privy to all kinds of information."

Nathan looked up at him.

"I mean, of course I can't get involved," Roland said. "But I can answer questions, you know? Share my knowledge, to anybody who asks." He paused, then frowned.

"Anybody," he repeated, staring at Nathan. "At all. Even a dull-witted newbie looking to go get himself killed because he's too thick to take a hint."

"What good would it do? Adams would probably break my legs to stop me following him."

"You need to man up. Look, you feel bad about what happened to your friend, yeah? And you'd probably like it very much if she'd never been hurt, and you could live your life like a normal human being, huh?"

Nathan nodded.

"Right." Roland grabbed a black denim jacket from a hook on the wall and put it on. "You're coming with me."

"Where?" Nathan pulled on his own jacket and followed him out the door.

"It's a surprise."

Roland led Nathan to a maintenance hatch near some old subway vents. He opened it and climbed a ladder down into the darkness.

"Don't worry," Roland said. "Nothing to be afraid of but the shadows. But they won't hurt you as long as you don't shut your eyes."

"You're kidding, right?"

Roland dropped the last two feet from the ladder onto a concrete floor. "Huh? Oh, sure. Probably. Come on, this way."

Roland shone a flashlight down a long grey tunnel and began walking until they reached an old steel door. He ignored the red words reading DANGER: NO ACCESS and pushed the door open. This led into another tunnel, lit by buzzing halogen bulbs. Roland put his flashlight away and the two of them walked along the tunnel.

Nathan saw tracks along the ground through an opening up ahead. They had come out into an old subway tunnel. People gathered around fire barrels, all wearing dirty, worn clothing and looking like they were in need of a decent meal. They backed away from Nathan, but seemed to relax once they saw Roland.

"Who are these people?" Nathan looked around at the tired, wary eyes watching him. Some of the oldest looked ancient, while the youngest included toddlers and even newborns. One woman, sitting on an old wooden crate and nursing an infant wrapped in a cloth blanket, looked away when he met her gaze.

"You know that war we had here, the one that drove the reborn out of New York?"

"Yeah."

"These are the people who got left behind. They call themselves The Lost."

Roland stepped around an old man sleeping under a coat. "See, not everyone in the war was a fighter. Some were just sympathizers; those mostly got rounded up by Dorian and killed."

The tunnel fell further into disrepair as they walked. Walls were cracked and broken; old rusted grates looked up to the night sky.

"Then there are people who knew about the real world, the one which most people ignore because it terrifies them too damn much to think it might be real. They knew enough to be put in danger. With the reborn gone it was left to people with no power, no past-life memories, no training, and no hope worth a damn to try and keep the mundanes safe."

Roland stopped to light a cigarette off a fire barrel. "That plan lasted all of five minutes. Predators like vampires and ghouls prefer mundane prey. They're less able to defend themselves, and they're too scared people will think they're crazy to go to the police. The people you're looking at have all been victims, one way or another, of Dorian and his minions. Life up above gets too tough for them. They get scared, weak, and become easier prey. They come here, where they can at least keep an eye on each other."

"Kind of late for so many to be awake."

"They sleep in shifts; there are always a lot of people awake."

"Can't you do anything?"

"Like what? Spot them some spare change, bring a few sandwiches down, sure. And when I come down here, someone like Eli is less likely to take a crack in case they get me and violate my sanctuary; but I told you, I can't get involved. These people don't need charity, kid."

"They need a hero."

Roland laughed. "What? Hell no. That's the last thing they need. I'm gonna try not to get all Tina Turner on you here, but I wanna show you this."

He led Nathan into a large circular chamber cut from natural rock. He pointed to a large grotto in the wall, an alcove adorned with old, red curtains. A cluster of candles stood vigil below photographs, notes, letters, patches of clothing, locks of hair, watches, jewelry, and other small mementos, all pinned to the wall. Nathan stepped into the alcove and, staring at the gathered pieces, began to understand.

"Everything you're looking at represents someone these people have lost." Roland leaned on an armchair. "If you're thinking of being added to the collection, go right ahead. But if you ask me, you should do like you said and go back to your own life. Because once you start down this path, it's nothing but blood and darkness."

Nathan turned and looked at Roland, each of the mementos etched into his memory. "That's why you're showing me this? To convince me not to help?"

"And well he should," came a cracked voice.

An elderly woman, hunched over and leaning on a walking stick, inched her way from a small doorway. She was wearing an "I ❤ NY" t-shirt underneath a grey button-down cardigan.

"Been years since we had one like you," she said. "But not too long that we don't remember. The reborn abandoned us, left us here to rot, and they can't help us now."

"I'm different," Nathan said. "I'm able to stay and fight."

This wasn't just a murder case to solve, not anymore. These were living people who needed help.

"Fight? Ha!" The old woman fixed Nathan with faded eyes. "C'mere, lemme look at you."

She stepped up to Nathan and pushed his chin back with her walking-stick, then shone a flashlight in his face.

"Gah!" Nathan backed away, rubbing his blinded eyes. "What the hell?"

The old woman sighed. "Not even the sense to stop someone near-blinding you with a light stuck in your face. No, you won't do."

Roland smirked. "Nathan, this is Libby. She's been here longer than anyone."

Libby gave a chuckle and started on her way back to the curtained doorway. “No, no good at all.”

As his vision began to clear, Nathan looked past Libby and into her room. Inside he saw old Broadway posters and a sword mounted on the wall. He frowned and walked toward it. The sword gleamed, the candlelight dancing across the steel. The hilt was cruciform, decorated with a stylized bird surrounded by flames.

“Don’t go thinking there’s anything there for you, boy,” Libby said. “Those’re my things, and we might not look like much down here, but we look out for our own. You wouldn’t get ten feet if you tried to rob me.”

“That sword. It’s beautiful.”

“It is. As was its last owner. We were sad to lose her.”

“Was she a friend?”

“Hmm? Oh, yes. Good friend.” She turned and looked up at Nathan. “You don’t really want to be fighting, do you?”

“I want a quiet life. A family.” The more he said it, the less it felt true.

Libby’s face fell. “Don’t we all? Well, my advice is, if you’ve got the chance to have one, take it. Don’t become like us. We never had that chance.”

“Because there was no one to fight for you,” Nathan said, softly. “Adams will. I’ll tell Adams about this place. I’ll tell him there’s something here worth fighting for.”

He turned and walked back the way he and Roland had come.

Chapter Ten

THEY LEFT THROUGH THE SUBWAY TUNNEL ITSELF. It emerged onto a disused set of Amtrak rails, through a place commonly known to vagrants, graffiti artists, and urban explorers as Freedom Tunnel. The irony of the name wasn't lost on Nathan.

"What happens now?" Roland asked.

"Now I find Adams," Nathan said, heading up into the park. "I'll tell him about the people here."

Roland stopped him as he was getting into his car. "Look, Nathan, Adams isn't the man you think he is. He's no hero. He was an asshole during the war; he's still an asshole today."

"He was a lot younger then. People change."

Roland shrugged.

"Do you really want me to quit and forget all this?"

"What I want is a nice scotch and a good Cuban cigar. What you want is up to you. I just wanted you to know exactly what you were risking before you go any further. No shame in deciding this isn't the life for you."

"And all that talk about me needing to man up?"

"That doesn't mean you should dive head first into a war." Roland's face softened. "If you think you can help, gear up and start kicking some ass, fuck some shit up. If you want to make things work with your girlfriend and not have your friends think you're a nut job, then walk away and let Adams and his crew do what they came here to do. No one will think less of you, so stop trying to act like you're offended every time Adams turns you down."

Roland let Nathan get into the car, and then he said, "If it makes you feel any better, Libby likes you."

"Terrific. My biggest fan is a crazy mole woman who lives in a subway."

Nathan spent the next few hours driving through the streets of the city, until he was steering on instinct and memory. He had repeated the turns and stops enough that he knew exactly when the lights would change, and when his next turn was coming. Something about the monotony was comforting. The dull drone of repetition was safe.

At one time, the towers of glass and steel had been nothing but wood, brick, and mortar. Nathan remembered a time like that. Without warning, the memories came to him. The image of ancient streets and people appeared in his vision. He'd been in New York before.

A sudden shout broke his reverie and he stopped his car, ignoring a blaring horn behind him. He looked across the street and saw a man pulling a young woman down an alley. His senses were heightened by the flash of memory he'd just experienced, and he heard the man snarling just before he saw him press her against the wall and lower his face to her throat.

Vampire!

Nathan jumped out of the car, taking his sports bag with him, and ran to the alley. He barreled into the vampire, knocking him away from his prey. Nathan staggered to keep his balance and turned, using the force of the spin to fuel a follow-up punch which caught the creature off guard. He fell back and braced himself against the wall, flashing his fangs at Nathan before escaping into the street.

"Are you okay?" he asked the girl.

She looked about sixteen, though she was wearing a short pvc skirt and a corset-style top. Her face was caked in too much make-up. She was bleeding from the bite wound on her neck, but looked up at Nathan and nodded. He ran after her attacker.

The vampire appeared from around the corner as Nathan left the alley, striking him right across the jaw. Nathan hit the ground hard and the vampire stepped over him toward the girl, his eyes now hungry and dilated with red and yellow streaking out from their centers.

Nathan shouted at the girl to run, but she lay still, looking up at her attacker in a daze. He reached into his bag and grabbed one of the bottles of holy water he'd bought. He threw it and it smashed against the side of the vampire's head. Nathan waited for the smoking and burning to start, but it never did.

The vampire laughed and turned back to Nathan. "You gotta be kidding me," he said, licking his fangs.

Holy water doesn't work, of course not. Nathan rolled aside as the vampire tried to kick him. He reached into his sports bag again and found the flare gun under an empty thermos. The vampire pulled Nathan to his feet, and he slammed his knee into the vampire's groin. He doubled over in pain.

Nathan loaded the flare gun and fired. The burning red flare stuck on the vampire's shirt, searing into his flesh. He shrieked and clawed at the flare, though he only managed to burn his hands and spread the flames to his arms. Nathan hurried to shield the girl as the vampire flailed. The fire spread quickly, causing his flesh to blister and peel. Nathan held an arm up to turn the girl's face away. He watched the vampire burn until it stopped thrashing and its body melted into a putrid puddle of bubbling slime.

Fire worked. That was good to know.

Nathan drove the girl to the hospital and handed her over to a nurse before collapsing onto a bench. Exhaustion took over and he soon found himself dreaming.

Nathan felt the warm touch of skin against his own. Gentle hands held him, caressing him slowly in stark contrast to the eager lips against his neck. He kept his eyes closed, enjoying the tactile sensation of his lover's motions. A deep voice, not his own, whispered declarations of love.

Nathan opened his eyes.

A handsome man, chin and jaw lightly dusted with stubble, returned his gaze.

The shock almost caused Nathan to wake, and the image began to blur, but he recalled Roland's advice and knew that this was a memory of another time. He needed to see this if he wanted to understand what was happening to him.

Nathan felt the sensations of the memory come more strongly, more precisely. His body felt different. He felt smaller; his arms were slender, his hair was long. His lover moved between his legs.

Holy shit, I'm a woman.

"Katherine," the man said. "Marry me?"

"I can't."

"We can't miss this chance again." The man had a strong, refined English accent.

"Malcolm." Katherine stroked his face. "A couple more months won't hurt." Her accent was different; Irish, maybe?

"You're afraid he'll come after us again, aren't you?" Malcolm sat up in the bed. It was made of rich mahogany and had linen curtains hanging around the sides.

"He might. We can't be sure. Only way we can be sure is to go after him first."

"I'd like, just once, to not have to think about fighting or monsters or searching through the shadows, protecting people who'll never know what we do."

Katherine ran her fingers through Malcolm's hair. "So would I."

Images shifted and months passed by in memory. Nathan found himself seeing things through Katherine's eyes as she ran toward a horse-drawn carriage. He recognized the London streets.

Malcolm was by Katherine's side, holding her hand. He carried a pistol in his other hand and they were scared.

The man they'd spoken of before had found them. Again. Nathan couldn't recall complete details about him, but he was afraid, just knowing he was close by. A gunshot rang out and the carriage driver fell from his seat.

Malcolm turned and fired his pistol without aiming. Katherine screamed when she saw a police constable fall to his knees. Malcolm dropped his pistol, turning pale.

Men appeared from all around, grabbing the couple and pulling them apart. Two figures approached from an alley. One wore a cape and a hood which cast a dark shadow over his face. Though she couldn't see his eyes, Katherine knew he was looking at her. Next to him stood a man in a top hat and wearing fine clothes.

"Vincent Dorian, you treacherous dog! Gods damn you! Damn you to hell!"

Dorian seemed younger in this memory. This must have been before he joined the Council of Chains. The man in the hood waved his men on, a mix of London police and dirty henchmen. They grabbed Katherine. She watched helplessly as a constable struck Malcolm across the back of the head with a truncheon. He collapsed and men carried him off. Dorian looked away as the hooded man's henchmen dragged Katherine away, screaming.

Four men brought Katherine to a narrow, dimly lit street and pushed her onto her back in the alcove of a butcher's shop. One of the men pressed her arms back, while another knelt between her legs. The other two kept watch, eagerly waiting their turn. Her heart raced. Her breath caught in her throat, and she felt like she might pass out from fear.

She pushed through the fear, feeding on the adrenaline coursing through her body.

Katherine locked eyes with the man holding her down; he froze. "Let me go or you all die," she commanded.

Someone yelled to ignore her, and she felt the man between her legs pulling and cutting at her petticoat with a knife. They had their warning. *No mercy.*

Katherine locked her thighs around the head of the man between her legs and wrenched hard, snapping his neck. The man holding her down panicked and loosened his grip enough for her to break free, snatch the knife tucked into his boot, and jam it into his abdomen. She stood and advanced on the last two thugs. They tried to run, but she was faster and had lifetimes of experience in killing when she had to.

Right now, she didn't have to. She wanted to.

The men died easily, too easily to satisfy her. This was a life she'd tried to put behind her, a world she'd wanted to forget. But *he* kept dragging her into it. And Dorian had helped him find her. She cursed herself for trusting him. Katherine ran, disappearing into the night.

Over the next several days, she tried to find Malcolm. She scoured the streets, bribed constables and prison guards, but no one knew where he was being held. It was on the day of his execution that she was finally able to see him one last time.

Disguised, she watched as the man she loved was brought to the gallows on charges of murder. She'd been ready to leap to his aid, to cut down any who dared stop her. Before she could draw her blade, Malcolm saw her and recognized her, even through her dirt-smeared face and dyed hair.

He smiled sadly and shook his head. She hesitated. Just for a moment. It was enough for her to miss her chance. Malcolm mouthed the words, "I love you," before the hangman did his work.

Katherine didn't cry or scream. She sank into the crowd and left, waiting only long enough to see Malcolm's legs stop kicking and silently pray that his soul moved on quickly to its rest.

She had to leave London. She needed to train, to contact old allies. Dorian had helped bring her back into the conflict, unwittingly re-forging her into a weapon. As she had done lifetimes before, she would fight.

But first, she had to re-learn all that she knew.

Time passed in the memories. Nathan saw all of Europe and Asia through Katherine's eyes as she traveled, venturing deeper and deeper into the supernatural world. Katherine trained with every weapon and in every fighting style she could find. Nathan felt her pain, both in her heart and in the injuries she sustained fighting men and monsters. He felt her strength and knowledge flow through him.

Several years later Katherine was on a ship on her way to America. Word had spread that Dorian had joined the Council of Chains and traveled to New York to serve them there. It was 1829 when she arrived. The sights, sounds, and smells were brand new. Even then the city was an urban sprawl to rival London or Paris.

Katherine took up residence in a townhouse near Central Park, posing as a wealthy, but young, widow. She kept her real name and made herself known in the city for her fondness of art and music, becoming a figurehead of society. She wanted Dorian to know she was there and that she had come for him.

Over time, she became more than just a society figure. She helped found charities to care for the poor and infirm and protected people from monsters prowling the streets. In supernatural circles she became known as a guardian, a respected member of the New York Conclave. She eventually gained enough status to come to earn the attention, and grudging respect, of the Council of Chains.

They arranged for her to meet their newest, brightest member. Vincent Dorian.

"I must say I'm surprised you haven't tried to kill me yet," Dorian said.

They were sharing a bottle of wine, sitting in a study decorated with dark wood furniture and smelling of fresh tobacco. It was customary for representatives of the Council of Chains to offer a drink to guests. Accepting the drink was a sign of trust that the host had not slipped poison into the glass.

Despite her feelings toward Dorian, Katherine knew he would obey the Council's instructions. If they'd wanted him to kill her she wouldn't have made it to the meeting alive.

"I decided to show you the kind of person I've been before," Katherine said. "Malcolm and I wanted a different life this time. Just once. And then you betrayed us. I wanted to show you the enemy you've made."

"You've made quite the name for yourself. Several rogue vampires have been dealt with. Ghoul attacks have stopped almost completely."

"Don't forget the cult I rooted out last week."

"Of course. They were quite a problem. You've been doing a lot of good since Malcolm died. I wonder if I'd kept your secret, would so many lives have been saved. If you really believe you're a reborn hero and you tried to turn your back on that, which of us is really the traitor?" Dorian said, and then took a long drink from his silver goblet.

Katherine narrowed her eyes and leaned across the table. "Don't think I can't kill you."

"You're here under the Council's hospitality. Such an attempt could make matters difficult for you and the rest of the Conclave."

"One day Dorian, in this life or the next, I will kill you." Katherine sat back and composed herself with several deep breaths.

"Why did you agree to this meeting?" Dorian refilled both their glasses. "It's no disrespect to the Council to refuse to meet with me, and you didn't come just to trade threats, surely?"

"I came to ask you why you handed us over like that. After all we've been through."

Dorian sneered. "You brought me into this world of yours, my dear. I never asked for it. Nor do I buy into your reborn ideology. You tell me you have memories of a time when we fought side by side. Well I tell you, no dream I've had felt real enough to make me believe that I have been another person in another life. There is only this life and the oblivion of death that follows." Dorian took a moment to calm himself. "I was offered an alternative. By our mutual acquaintance."

Katherine frowned. The Council of Chains often took on ordinary mortals to act as servants and low-level agents or soldiers. But to truly become one of them, a person had to be granted immortality by an existing member, or find a method of their own. Dorian had traded Malcolm and her for a way to live forever.

"You've grown older. Why haven't you taken advantage of this alternative?"

"I have my reasons. There is something I want before I claim immortality. Something you are going to help me get."

Katherine grimaced. "And why the bloody hell would I help you?"

"Because it's in the hands of someone who's a threat to both the Council and the Conclave, not to mention the clueless sheep that live in this city." Dorian clasped his hands together across his lap. "This individual possesses great power. He has been causing problems for the Council, seizing control of some of our lesser servants. The ghouls and animated dead so far, but he has also exhibited mastery over ghosts, spirits, and even the odd vampire and revenant. He has no small amount of talent in arcane areas, and we believe he is dabbling in acts of otherworldly summoning."

"A necromancer?" Katherine shivered. "Of course. The Council is mostly made up of undead creatures vulnerable to a necromancer's power. And none of your mortal agents would be able to stand up to him."

"If I'm going to prove myself to the Council and increase my station, it's my job to put a stop to his activities. A necromancer with his power can't go unchecked. He's too much of a risk to us. Much as it pains me to admit it, I need your help. Unless you would rather hold on to your grudge and let innocents continue to suffer and die at his hands simply to slight me?"

Katherine considered her goblet for a few moments, gazing into the dark red wine. She wanted nothing more than to drive a blade into Dorian's heart, but she couldn't. Firstly, because Dorian's guards hadn't let her bring her sword with her. And secondly, because she knew he was right. Stopping this necromancer was important. More important than her desire for revenge.

"Tell me his name."

"Thaddeus Morningway."

Chapter Eleven

A firm hand woke Nathan. He stirred. His back ached from spending the night on a hospital bench. A weathered face looked down at him. "Morning, son."

Mike handed Nathan a Styrofoam cup filled with coffee. He took a sip, burning his mouth in the process. It tasted awful. He sat up and made room for his dad to sit next to him.

"What time is it?" Nathan asked.

"After nine. Don't worry, I called your office, said you were laid-up in bed and I was looking after you. They said you'd missed two days' work already."

"Yeah."

"Well, it made it easier to spin a lie about you being too sick to move. Your boss didn't sound too happy though."

"How'd you know I was here?"

"Laura called," Mike said. "She told me you brought someone in to the hospital last night."

"Yeah, a girl. Is she okay?"

"Resting. Cops might wanna talk to you though. Looks like she was assaulted."

Nathan was relieved to know she was all right.

"It's been rough," Mike said. "Hasn't it?"

"What has?"

"Whatever it is you're going through. You should get some rest. Take another couple of days off work."

Nathan's mind was still foggy from the dream. "I feel like I'm losing my mind. Did Laura … is she here?"

"She's at home. When we spoke she said a colleague had called to tell her about you."

Nathan ran that one through his head for a moment. She'd called his father instead of coming to see him herself. He was losing her. Maybe he'd already lost her. Was it too late to fix the mess he'd made? *Wait.* She was supposed to be on duty last night. *She wouldn't have lied to me, would she?*

Mike stood and stretched, tucking his hands into the pockets of his green button-down cardigan. "Let's get some breakfast. You feel like pancakes?"

When Nathan was a boy, whenever he'd had a bad day at school, or had hurt himself falling, again, from the tree in their yard, his mother would cook him pancakes.

The pancakes at the diner he and his father walked to weren't as good as his mother's, but they smelled the same, and all at once Nathan was back in their family home in Queens, sunlight beaming in through the kitchen window. His mother pouring an extra helping of maple syrup over his pancakes while his father, dressed in his old uniform, his hair a sandy blond, free from any gray, waved goodbye to go to work. He was a picture of the man Nathan had wanted to be, the man he had tried to be. It was a good memory. One Nathan liked to keep for times like this.

They'd been eating quietly for several minutes when Nathan spoke. "I think I've made a big mistake."

Mike raised his eyebrows and set down his knife and fork.

"I'm involved in something." Nathan laid his hands down on the table to steady them. His actions the night before would not go unnoticed. Even without a body for the police to identify, Dorian would find out that a vampire in his city had been taken out. There was no turning back now.

"I killed a man last night."

Nathan froze, waiting for the first disappointed, disbelieving yells to come. He'd never been able to keep secrets from his father for long, even when he and Cynthia had started spending more time together, following investigations in the news.

The yelling didn't happen. Mike sat back and nodded calmly, rubbing his chin with one hand, revealing enough of his wrist for Nathan to see the old burn scars which ran down his right arm.

"He was trying to hurt the girl," Mike said.

Nathan nodded.

"And you stopped him."

"Yeah, I did."

"Then if the police ask you about it, we can tell them the truth."

"They won't. I don't think they'll find . . . well, you know."

Mike frowned, looking puzzled, but nodded and went back to his pancakes.

"Dad?" Nathan watched and waited for some response, anything to suggest how Mike was feeling. His father looked up at him and smiled.

"You've got yourself into some bad things," he said. "Haven't you?"

Nathan nodded while chewing his food.

"This isn't like last year when you sent the tip to the police about that girl's body in Central Park, is it?"

"No," Nathan replied.

"Your mother and me, we fought a bit about the amount of time I spent working. But she knew I loved the work. And much as I wanted to always be there for you both, the job was my duty and I had to put food on the table. She understood. Sure, there were times I got scared, thought I'd get myself killed and leave you both alone with no one to look after you. And those times, you know, I did wonder if it was all worth it. Or if I should just transfer maybe to arson investigation, or open up the bar like I'd always wanted."

"Why didn't you?" Nathan asked. "If you wanted to open the bar all this time, why wait until now?"

"It was gonna be my reward, you know?" Mike gulped back a mouthful of coffee. "Something just for me. I guess what I'm saying is, son, sure you want to do right for your family and friends; sure you want a good life. But the world doesn't work like that all the time. Sometimes you need to remind yourself of that. No matter how hard it is, some things just have to be done."

Mike scratched at his shoulder, where the burns had been the worst. Most of the sensation he had left across parts of his back was a dull ache or an itch that just wouldn't go away. He never complained, though. The only thing Nathan had ever seen his dad complain about was not being able to go back to work after he'd been burned. And even that he took in stride.

"I understand, Dad. Thanks."

After breakfast, they walked back to the hospital where Nathan gave a statement to the police. The girl had discharged herself before the police arrived. Listening to conversations and managing to get some information from the uniformed officers, Nathan learned that she'd given her name as Sally Brown. She had insisted she didn't want to press charges or speak to any cops.

She had left a note for Nathan, a folded piece of paper. On it, she had written *Thank you.*

Nathan left out any mention of the girl's attacker having fangs or melting into a goopy sludge when set on fire. He told them he'd seen the girl being assaulted and the attacker ran off when he shouted at him. Nothing the girl had said to the doctors or hospital staff seemed to contradict his story.

After meeting with the police, Nathan walked back to his car with his father.

A man in a suit approached them, taking off a pair of sunglasses. "Rough night?"

It was Powell, the detective who questioned Nathan after he brought Cynthia to the hospital.

"Good morning, Detective," Nathan said. "I already gave my statement. I'm about to give my dad a ride home, so I'm kind of in a hurry."

"I understand." Powell put his hand against the door of the car. "You know I got a call from the officers who came down when the hospital called this one in. Looks like you're a hero now, huh?"

"Detective Powell, can I please get into my car?"

"She had bite marks, didn't she? On her neck. Right about here." He pointed to his throat. "All bruised and torn. Not the first time I've heard of that."

"I'm sorry, Detective. I really don't remember much. It was late, and I just wanted to make sure she got to a hospital."

"Of course, which is why you took her half across town instead of calling an ambulance."

"I wasn't really thinking clearly. My girlfriend works here, so it was the first place to come to mind."

"Or you were running from something. What was it? Look, there have been a lot of rumors of some kind of cult activity in the city lately. I'm looking into it, but I keep getting stonewalled. You seem to be getting yourself caught up in something here, and it stinks. I checked your record. You previously had a couple of trespassing charges that were dropped. Your bosses think you're a bit of a freak, always looking up old death records and such. Then your friend at the medical examiner's office is assaulted at the same time those people break into the morgue. Now I find you bringing in a woman who's got a bite mark on her neck."

"You called my work?"

"They were a little reluctant to talk, but it looks like you've been on the edge of a lot of strange things lately. And yesterday, my lieutenant told me to drop any line of investigation on you. Now how do you suppose that happens?"

"I'm afraid I have no idea what's going on, Detective."

"I just want to know, Shepherd, are you with me or against me?"

"I'm not against you."

Mike approached the car. "Nathan, everything okay?"

"Everything's fine, Dad. Just helping Detective Powell here."

Mike nodded and climbed into the car. Powell stepped aside and Nathan got in. Powell leaned in close at the window. "There's been another death, like the ones before."

Nathan frowned.

"Mouth wide open, stretched too far, face all twisted up like they died in horrible pain." Powell held his gaze until Nathan looked away.

"Father of four," Powell continued. "Out for dinner with his family. Just went to get them a cab and some guy pulls him into an alley. By the time the wife goes looking, he's dead. She found him on the street; all dried up like the others, people just walking by like it wasn't even there. If you know something, or you're involved somehow, it's better you tell me now."

Nathan couldn't look Powell in the eye. A woman and her four children, with no idea what killed her husband or why. It made him sick and scared. "I'm sorry, Detective. I told you, I'm not against you."

He drove away from the hospital and turned onto a street to head up to his father's neighborhood.

"You should've told him if you know something, son."

Nathan's neck ached. He wanted more coffee. And a hot shower. "I don't."

"You know more than he does. I can see that much in your eyes."

"He can't help. The police can't do anything about this."

"But you can."

"No. Maybe. I know some people who can help, but I need to convince them to listen to me."

After leaving his father at the door to his apartment building, Nathan drove on, swinging around to head back to the south of Manhattan. He called Ben.

"Hey, Ben. It's Nathan. Things just got serious. We have some work to do. I need you to bring me some things. Write this down and meet me after dark."

They arranged to meet in a parking garage close to where the soul eater's latest victim had been found.

While Nathan waited at the parking garage, he unpacked a number of items from his sports bag, including his flashlight. He tucked the flare gun, his five remaining flares, and a small penknife into his pockets.

Ben pulled his car next to Nathan's and got out.

"Did you bring the stuff?" Nathan asked.

He held up the camcorder and handed Nathan a Dictaphone. "What's all this for?"

"There's a thing killing people. We're going to find it and tell the people who want it dead where it is."

"What's this got to do with Cynthia?"

"There are other people who might want the creature dead, but they don't want outsiders like you and me getting involved. What they did to Cynthia was a warning to me to stay out of this."

Ben nodded, a determined smile settling on his face. "But fuck them, basically?"

"Basically."

"And the recording equipment?"

"Evidence. I know Laura won't believe any of this if we tell her, but I want her to know. I'm through keeping it from her. We'll do this, video the creature, and when it's over we show her."

"Sounds like a good plan. What's this thing we're looking for, and how dangerous is it?"

"They call it a soul eater. But we're staying out of its way. The people who can stop it need information that only I can get, but their leader is a bit hard to convince of anything. I need more information before he'll listen."

"Why is it only you that can find this out?"

They walked out of the parking garage and across the street. Memories of Nathan's past life came to him easily; he could feel the soft material of a dress he had once worn when he was Katherine.

Down the street, he saw a construction site where the foundations for a new office building were currently being laid. Images of an older building, a 19th century townhouse, overlaid his vision. Thaddeus Morningway's home.

"Because in another life I killed monsters."

Ben and Nathan walked toward the wooden walls set up to keep people out of the construction site.

Nathan's memories of Katherine's life were vivid, but incomplete. He knew that she had gone with Dorian to Morningway's home to confront him, and it seemed like a good place to start looking for clues. He had found Morningway's Manhattan address in the books from the library, and this construction site was right on top of it. An on-site death shortly before Miranda Grange was killed led to construction being halted while a police investigation was being carried out. To add to that, the building work was being carried out by Murdoch & Sullivan.

If Dorian knew that Morningway summoned the soul eater, and his puppet company was in charge of the construction work right on top of the remains of Morningway's old home, why hadn't he already had the soul eater killed? He'd been in control of New York for over a decade. In that time he would have had plenty of opportunities to destroy it.

Ben used a pair of bolt cutters to cut through the chains securing the door in the wooden wall. "If you're some reincarnated monster hunter, why do you need me?"

"If I get hurt it'd be nice to be brought to a hospital." They slipped in through the gate. "Besides, if for some reason I don't make it, someone's got to get this information to where it can be used."

"Why wouldn't you make it? You said we were staying out of this thing's way."

"Night time. Vampires. They work for the guy who runs the city. And they don't like me."

"Why not?"

"I killed one last night." They made their way past a large excavator and toward a collection of pre-fab office units. "You're not freaking out?"

"I know you. You'd never lie about something like this, especially not after what happened to Cynthia." Ben reached into his coat pocket and drew out a revolver. "Which is why I came prepared."

Nathan stared at the gun. "Okay, uh, Ben do you have a permit for that thing?"

"It used to belong to my dad," he said. "I figure if I have to use it the last thing I'll be worried about is a permit."

"And you know how to use it?"

"Sure do. Lead the way."

"What about everything you said about helping me do this the right way?"

"I'm all for doing things the right way. But I don't want to be caught off guard if the wrong way decides to take a shot at us."

Nathan scanned the building site. Floodlights stood connected to generators, all turned off. The only light reaching them was cast down from surrounding buildings, covering everything in a faint gray sheen. He shone his flashlight over the chalk outline where the body had been found. It had been a dry few days, leaving the outline untouched. A small excavator sat nearby, its bucket hanging over a pit.

Nathan and Ben approached the edge. The workers had uncovered something buried deep beneath the streets.

Under the sand and broken rock Nathan could see worked stone, possibly granite. There was a hole large enough for a grown man to fit through.

Nathan's light shone against more stone surfaces below, but it was hard to tell anything from above ground. He knelt down and held his hand out. There was definitely an airflow coming from somewhere. And something else. Like a steady current, a tide washed against his senses, urging him to stay away. He frowned and reached into the hole, through the wave. The more he resisted the easier it became, until finally the tide faded away. He remembered what Cadence told him about places having their own energy. Perhaps places of supernatural activity had their own way to keep people from getting too curious. Yes. That sparked something in his memory.

"What is it?" Ben asked.

"Looks like an old basement or cellar," Nathan said. "Must have been covered over some time after the older building was destroyed. Strange that it wasn't excavated or filled in earlier."

Perhaps mundane people found it hard, almost impossible, to push through that tide of energy? It could explain how vampires and other creatures walked the streets with such ease. The human mind was trained to ignore it. The question was, was that to protect the supernatural? Or a survival instinct humanity had developed?

Ben blinked, his eyes briefly glazing over. "What're you talking about?"

"Huh?"

"It's just concrete. There's nothing there."

Nathan grabbed Ben's hand and held it over the hole. "Ignore what you're brain is telling you. Just . . . I don't know, let yourself feel."

Ben snorted. "Sure thing, Obi Wan."

As Ben leaned over the pit he started to flex his fingers. Nathan felt the flow of energy pass through him, down his arm and into Ben. Ben's eyes widened. He shook his head and tried to pull away, but Nathan held him there.

"What the hell is this?"

"Your first step into a larger world, young Skywalker. There are things that don't want you to see them. They've got ways of hiding, but you can see through them if you let yourself." He let go of Ben's hand.

"Right." Ben rubbed his arms, shivering. "What do you think happened here?"

A sudden sensation of heat wrapped around Nathan. Heat and choking smoke. For a moment he was unable to breathe and he had to remind himself it was just a memory, that it couldn't harm him.

"There was a fire," he said. "The building burned down, then was built over. If the soul eater got out before, there must be another way to the surface."

Nathan found some nylon rope near the site and tied one end off on the excavator before dropping the other into the hole. He let the flashlight drop into the hole, onto its side, and started to lower himself in.

Ben grabbed his shoulder. "You sure about this?"

"The soul eater hunts at night. Odds are it's not here."

"And if it is?"

"Run."

Ben followed Nathan down and turned on his own flashlight. They found themselves in an empty cellar. The walls where lined with wine racks, most of which were empty, the wood rotten and cracked. Some of them held empty or broken bottles, but Nathan did find an intact bottle of red wine, covered in dust, with the year 1796 printed on it.

He smiled, holding back a triumphant laugh. It was the right place. It had to be. They were in Morningway's cellar.

A door hung open. They ventured into a wide hall filled with rubble where walls or stairs should have been. Nathan's heart pounded as he saw the cellar in his memory, as it had once been, lit by oil lamps on the walls. Fine rugs lay under his feet instead of bare stone. The scent of incense drifted through the air. He found himself copying the movements from his memory, one foot forward, his weight centered in case he needed to shift his stance.

The old servants' quarters were up ahead.

Ben shone his light in each of the six rooms lined up on the right. "Jesus," he said. "I think I see bones. Did they just leave people down here?"

Nathan ducked under thick grey cobwebs as he reached a set of double doors. He wiped the dust, revealing ebony woodwork and faded brass door handles. The wood showed signs of fire damage. The brass had warped from heat. His fingers came away black with soot as he eased the door open and stepped into the chamber.

"Nathan," Ben said. "These rooms … they have chains in them."

Nathan turned back and looked at Ben, frowning. As he thought about it, his recollection began to change. They weren't servants' rooms. They were cells. This was where Morningway kept his test subjects.

"Come here," he said. "I think we've reached the spot."

Ben stepped up and they shone their lights around the room. Nathan scraped some soot and dust from the floor with his boot, revealing copper lines laid into the marble. He brushed away enough to reveal a pentacle, with settings for candles at each point of the star. The walls of the pentagonal room were lined with the remains of shelves and at the head of the pentacle stood a black marble altar. He examined the old iron manacles built into it. They were thick and strong, though rust had worn into them.

The ceiling was lined with flues for letting out smoke. Empty settings, which once held oil lamps and coal braziers, lay beneath them. In one corner the wall had been broken through into a tunnel.

Nathan knelt to take a closer look. It was large enough that at least two people could crawl through side by side. A bundle of old clothes lay further inside.

"Wait," Ben said. "Did you . . . ? I think I heard something."

Nathan crawled in toward the bundle. It looked like an old dress, though he could see hardened leather showing through tears in the material.

"Nathan, maybe we should go."

An old pistol lay close to the dress, near a leather belt holding several rusted knives. A hand lay over a face. The flesh had long since rotted away or been eaten by scavengers, leaving only worn bone.

Gently, Nathan lifted the hand and arm out of the way and pointed his light at the hollow skull. She still had some hair left, clutching to her head in spots where the skin hadn't been completely removed. Something in his stomach tried to scramble up his throat, but he swallowed it back down.

He touched the cheekbone of the skull. Instantly he felt his lungs heaving and his skin burning. He pulled away and took deep, slow breaths. These were Katherine O'Reilly's remains.

Nathan looked into her empty eye sockets, half expecting to blink and see her smiling at him. But she hadn't smiled for a very long time before she died. She'd held a great sorrow within her, all the way into her last moments. Nathan wondered how much of that pain had carried over after death and whether he still held any of it.

"Nathan?"

"Hold on. There's more to the tunnel. I want to see what's up here."

He crawled past Katherine's remains. As he crawled, a low rumble grew. A nearby subway train. He saw a mound of fallen rubble up ahead. A small opening looked out into a round tunnel. This must have been how the soul eater got to the surface. An escape tunnel Morningway had constructed in the event of his work being discovered.

The tunnel design was the same as the old Beach Pneumatic Transit line, the first conceptual subway system in New York. Built back in the late nineteenth century, it failed due to a lack of funding. However, the line had been built much further south.

Perhaps this was an earlier construction. A prototype tunnel or a later attempt to continue the project. Whatever it was, its construction must have disturbed Morningway's escape tunnel. Perhaps the workers disturbed the soul eater in the process. A mysterious death and rumors of haunted tunnels would certainly cause investors to back out.

"Ben! Come down here!"

He arrived behind Nathan, wiping cobwebs from his shirt. "Got some video of the rooms back there. What's this?"

Nathan pulled himself through the small opening and tumbled down onto the floor of the tunnel. Ben followed, landing more steadily.

"Part of the old pneumatic transit tunnels, I think," he said. "The soul eater probably uses them to get up to the streets, nesting in the old cellar. I bet the construction workers disturbed it, and it killed one of them. Somewhere here there must be a way through to the sewers or the subway system."

He scanned the area and started walking along the tracks. It was pitch black aside from the beams from their flashlights.

"Only problem is Adams and the others think the soul eater's been carving out a hunting ground around its lair. But this thing's not an animal. It's intelligent. It's hunting far from where it sleeps, so it won't draw attention to the place where it's vulnerable."

"Clever," Ben said.

Something chilled Nathan's flesh. His breath turned to fog in the air. The temperature had fallen suddenly. "You said you heard something before. What was it?"

"Sort of a jingling sound. I thought maybe it was something moving in the breeze from the surface."

A faint clink echoed in the darkness. Nathan moved his flashlight around the tunnel. For a moment, he thought he saw a shape, but it quickly vanished to the sound of sudden jangling. He started and dropped his flashlight. It landed front-first and the bulb smashed. He swore and grabbed Ben's arm, pointing the flashlight down the tunnel. Nothing.

Just the ringing echo of jingling metal, flowing like a heartbeat all around them.

"We're in trouble," Nathan said.

Chapter Twelve

BEN BOLTED DOWN THE TUNNEL, DROPPING THE recording equipment. Nathan ran, following Ben's light. They kept running until they reached an old station platform underneath Murray Street. They helped each other up onto the platform.

"These old tunnels run close to the sewer system," Nathan said.

From the darkness around them came a low, long rasp. In the dim light, Nathan saw a pile of rubble underneath a collapsed portion of the ceiling. He ran to it and started climbing; almost crying out in joy when he found that there was a hole at the top large enough for him to squeeze through.

"This way!"

He came out into a main sewer line and slipped, falling onto the maintenance walkway. Ben came through after him, and Nathan had to roll to get out of the way. He fell again, down into the river of refuse. He shut his mouth tight and held his breath as his face was briefly submerged.

He clawed back onto his feet, wiping his face and gagging on the smell.

"Ugh. Ben, you okay?"

"Think I twisted my ankle when I fell."

"We have to keep moving," Nathan helped Ben to stand and all but dragged him down the sewer tunnel. "We should be able to reach the surface from here."

"Can't we kill it?"

"Need to find its phylactery. That's the source of its power. It'll be wearing it."

There was the sound of jingling metal again. Service lights ran all the way down the tunnel, so they didn't need Ben's torch to see. He looked back but saw nothing following them.

The metal jingled again and Nathan slowly followed the source of the sound. Right above his head.

A snarling face stared down at him. Yellow teeth showed through holes where the flesh had rotted away. Pale light glowed in its eye sockets and a ragged coat hung from its body.

Nathan wasn't sure where hanging pieces of dead flesh stopped and matted, filth-encrusted hair began. Mud and worse dripped onto him from the skeletal figure. It hung from the ceiling of the tunnel with ease, as though its body simply stuck to the brick.

The soul eater dropped, pinning Nathan on his back. He reached up with his left hand to try and defend himself, but the creature caught his wrist and drove black fingernails into Nathan's skin, pressing right against the bone. He cried out and struggled to get free.

"Mine now." The soul eater hissed as it bent over Nathan, straddling him. It smelled of mold and rancid meat.

A crack of thunder filled the tunnel and the soul eater jerked, falling away. Nathan scrambled away on his hands and knees as Ben hobbled closer, his father's revolver smoking in his hand.

Ben fired twice more, one shot striking the soul eater in the chest and the other ringing off the wall. It looked back at him, its one eyebrow twisting in rage.

"Just die!" Ben said and emptied the last three rounds; but it didn't fall.

"Move!" Nathan got up to run.

Ben dropped the revolver and ran as best he could on his injured foot. The soul eater let out a howl behind them.

Ahead Nathan saw a ladder set into a shallow alcove. "Come on!" He charged ahead and started climbing.

He reached the top and pushed on the manhole cover. Beneath him, Ben was breathing heavily. "Oh God, it didn't die."

Nathan looked down. Ben was clutching onto the ladder, shaking and leaning his head against a rung.

"Ben, stay with it. We're almost out. I just..." He heaved against the metal cover and it budged. He was able to use his shoulders to wedge the cover up and slide it to one side. "Got it!"

They climbed up and crawled out of the manhole. The soul eater was fast behind them. Its claws tore through Ben's jacket. Nathan balled his fist and smashed it across the jaw.

"Come on you sorry lump of bones," he said. "You're not finished with me yet."

The soul eater twisted its head around and snarled. Pus and flaking skin fell from where its jawbone was hanging loose.

Blood dripped from Nathan's knuckles. "Ben, run." Nathan stepped back, keeping his arms raised in defense. "Get out of here."

"What about you?"

"I'll be fine. Meet me at my place. Go!"

The soul eater sniffed the air as Ben ran.

Nathan punched it again and ran. "We're not done yet, death-breath."

It screeched and obliged him, bounding along behind him on all fours.

Nathan couldn't outrun the soul eater, and he couldn't fight it. He had nowhere to hide. He saw a late night drug-store up ahead and a desperate plan came to mind. Tucking his head under his arm, he jumped through the window.

Glass shattered as he fell through a cardboard display, rolling along the floor as he tucked himself into a ball to absorb the impact. Shards of glass cut his hands and face.

There weren't many people in the store. An older woman screamed and fell back against a stand of cosmetics. Two younger people, students from the look of them, backed away while the clerk on duty started shouting and swearing at Nathan.

Nathan crawled across the floor and pushed past the clerk. He found the store's panic button under the cash register and pressed it. As he did, the soul eater came crashing through the rest of the window.

Nathan ducked down behind the register and found the store clerk staring back at him, trembling. He was just a kid. Maybe eighteen. Nathan raised his finger to his lips to shush him and peered around the side of the counter.

The older woman huddled in a ball, hiding her face. Nathan couldn't see the soul eater but he heard the rustling of its clothing. *What the hell is making that noise?* He had to delay it, or scare it off. The cops would be on their way, but it was late and he couldn't be sure how long they'd be.

Someone screamed as something crashed to the ground. Nathan inched around the side of the register and saw the back of the soul eater climbing over a toppled set of shelves. In bright light, he could see that its coat was covered in small trinkets, from jewelry to ID cards and even finger bones. They had been sewn onto the coat, and caused the jingling sound it made as it moved.

They were trophies. Mementoes from each of its victims. The coat was covered in them.

Anger swallowed Nathan's fear.

The young man stepped between the soul eater and his female friend. He was pale and sweaty with fear, but he tried to swing a punch anyway. The soul eater caught the swing in one hand and wrenched downward. There was a popping sound and the boy dropped to the floor, screaming. The soul eater lowered itself over the boy and reached for his mouth. The girl screamed again and grabbed its arm. The soul eater swatted her aside, knocking her against a rack of magazines.

Nathan checked his flare gun. It was filled with excrement and sewer water. Useless. He searched behind the register and found an old golf club. It would have to do. He walked out from behind the register.

"Hey, pus-face! How about you try that with me?"

The soul eater looked up and snarled. It stood upright, standing at least half a head over Nathan on long, crooked legs. It stepped over the fallen shelves toward him.

Nathan swung the golf club, but the soul eater caught it in one hand and threw him back against the cash register. He pushed off from the counter and charged the soul eater. It grabbed him, turned with his momentum, and let go. Nathan smashed through the door of a refrigerator cabinet.

A broken chuckle greeted him as he climbed back to his feet. The soul eater waited for him, grinning. Nathan frowned. Was it toying with him? It cocked its head at him, as if sizing him up.

The bastard really is *intelligent. Shit.*

"What?" Nathan lifted the golf club again. "Got cold feet? Come on; don't chicken out on me now."

The soul eater leaped at him, its animal rage returning, teeth bared and claws reaching for him. It slammed him down onto the floor and clasped its hands around his throat.

"Mine! Mine!" Its dead white eyes locked with Nathan's, and he felt an ice cold familiarity. "Will not be taken!"

Nathan felt an uneasy dizziness and his vision began to blur. He reached up and grabbed hold of the jaw. With a hard pull, he tore the bone half off. The creature roared and released him. Coughing as he gulped in air, Nathan rolled away and climbed to his feet.

The soul eater re-attached its jaw with a sickening crunch as it stood. “Will pay,” it hissed.

Nathan was panting. He was tired, hurt, and so far, nothing had done more than slow the soul eater down a little. The people in the store had gathered behind him, placing him between them and the soul eater. He looked back at the four of them. The girl was cradling her friend in her lap. The old woman was crying, and the clerk stared in blank terror at what was happening.

Nathan turned back to the soul eater. “Come and get me.”

He ran at the creature, this time ducking when it tried to grab him. He tackled it around the waist and took it through the glass door of the store. They tumbled out into the street where the soul eater threw Nathan off and into the path of a car. The car skidded to a halt and there was the wail of a siren. Red and white lights lit the street. The soul eater was gone.

Someone shouted at Nathan to get up and put his hands on his head. When he didn’t, strong hands pulled him up and put his hands behind his back. He wasn’t sure exactly how long it all took; adrenaline was fading and being replaced by shock. He had begun to shake. The cops put him in the back seat of the patrol car, where he waited to be questioned.

Chapter Thirteen

NATHAN WAS KEPT IN AN INTERROGATION ROOM for hours, occasionally being offered more coffee or asked to go over the events one more time. Every time, it was a different officer. He sat the whole time in his sewage-soaked clothes. Unfortunately, while the police had let him shower, there were no clothes for him to change into. He would have to wait until morning to call someone and get them to bring clean clothes.

The door opened and Detective Powell walked in. He tossed a brown folder onto the table and stretched with a yawn. "Long night, huh?" He jerked his thumb at the door. "You want any coffee?"

Nathan shook his head no.

Powell sat across from him. "That's a hell of a story you're telling."

"Is it?"

Nathan had figured urban exploration was as good an excuse as any to be down in the sewers. He claimed to have disturbed a homeless person who became violent and attacked him, chasing him to the drugstore.

Powell opened the folder and handed Nathan some photographs. They were stills from security camera footage showing him coming through the drugstore window, soon followed by the soul eater. In the grainy images, it just looked like a tall, filthy person, though in some of the shots there was a real good look at its sunken, glowing eyes and skull-like face.

"That look like a homeless person to you? The witnesses say this guy attacked one of them, that you drove him off."

"I'm kind of fuzzy on it all, Detective."

"You know, Shepherd, it's getting really hard for me to think that it's just a coincidence that I keep running into you like this."

"Like what, Detective?"

"Let me see. We've got some kind of killer on our hands that's been leaving messed-up bodies for us to find. You've shown up to cause problems in two of those cases. Two assaults and you bring the victims to the hospital. Now you're having a fist fight with a guy in a grim reaper costume. This doesn't add up, Shepherd. I'm giving you one last chance to cooperate before I decide you're either responsible or an accomplice."

Nathan took a deep breath to steady his nerves. "Do you have any evidence to prove I was involved?"

Powell frowned and stood to lean across the table, pushing his face close enough to smell the stale donuts on his breath. "I've got you on public disorder, destruction of private property, trespassing on city property, and you're about a hair's breadth away from obstruction of justice."

"I've answered your questions as best I can, and I'll pay for the damage I caused to the store."

Powell walked to the door. "I'm going to keep you here until morning, when you can get someone to pay your bail. You've got until then to tell me what's really going on, or I swear to God, if there's so much as a hair of yours found on any of the victims, I'll put you away. You can look at those pictures a while longer too."

Powell left. Nathan pushed the pictures aside and folded his arms on the table, laying his head down. It was long after midnight, and he was exhausted. It didn't take him long to fall asleep.

Nathan dreamed of the soul eater's sneering face and being chased through dark tunnels. The dream changed and he found himself back in Morningway's cellar. Only this time it was properly lit by oil lamps, the walls free of burn marks. He was Katherine O'Reilly again, wearing a light, functional dress along with a harness which held knives and wooden stakes, most of which were already spent. Her sword was stained with blood, and behind her Vincent Dorian dispatched a walking corpse with an old Norse axe.

"We work well together," Dorian said, grinning.

"Don't get any ideas. I'm here to do a job. That's it."

"Wait." Dorian caught her arm as she advanced down the hall. "Before we go farther. I … I had hoped this wouldn't become an issue, that we'd find her somewhere in the house."

"Find who?"

"Elisabeth. Morningway's wife."

Katherine had done some research into Morningway. His wife was ill with consumption and not expected to live long. Katherine had expected her to be in her room, resting, and had counted on her being out of harm's way.

"You think she's in his workshop with him?" Katherine looked around the corner. It was clear.

"We have to save her." There was a tremble in Dorian's voice, and she felt a vague sympathy for him.

"Follow my lead. We move in fast, don't give him a chance to use her as a hostage. I engage Morningway and restrain him, you protect Elisabeth." She moved toward the broad ebony doors, Dorian close behind.

Katherine raised an amulet she wore around her neck and pointed it at the door. The spell was blunt, but effective. She uttered the command word, an ancient Latin phrase, and a wave of force left the amulet, striking the door. It hit the bolt and burst it out of the wood. The doors swung open and Katherine strode into the chamber beyond, sword held ready.

Thaddeus Morningway sat in a lotus position in the middle of a pentacle on the floor. Black candles surrounded him. He was reciting an ancient Sumerian incantation. He opened his eyes and smiled as he uttered the final words.

The power of the ritual flooded the room, forcing Katherine to her knees. Dorian tried to run past her, swinging his axe, but Morningway stood and lifted a hand. Dorian struck an invisible barrier which knocked him back onto the floor.

Morningway left the circle and walked to the altar at the back of the chamber. There, dressed only in a light undergarment, trembling, lay Elisabeth. Her skin was as pale as bleached bone and her lips were stained with blood from coughing. She murmured feeble cries for help, but Morningway shushed her, stroking her hair.

"All will be well, dear. Soon you shall be with me forever. Mine forever."

The air felt like a thick soup pressing down around Katherine. Dorian also seemed to be having trouble moving. "What have you done, Morningway?" Katherine demanded.

The necromancer smiled. "I invited some help."

The room darkened. Swirling clouds appeared in the air, spinning around. Wisps of black coalesced into hands and faces, all reaching out to grasp at the physical world.

"Good gods," Katherine said, "what are these beasts?"

"Soul eaters, dear lady," Morningway said, "and they are quite eager for a taste of life."

"Are you insane?" Dorian said. "Do you know what you've done?"

Morningway took the dragonfly pendant from around Elisabeth's neck and placed it around his own. "Mr. Dorian, I thought the Council would understand the potential here. Imagine never having to fear death again, your soul being kept safe for centuries, even millennia. Unending, until a way could be found to transcend the bonds of flesh."

"These creatures will never let you control them," Dorian said. "They'll consume you like they do everything else."

"Fool. I have no wish to control them."

Morningway raised his arms and began chanting. The cloud thickened and Katherine felt cold hands brushing over her body as they passed. Her sword lay just out of reach. If only she could move a little. The soul eaters swarmed around Morningway, their hold on the rest of the chamber weakening a little. She waited.

One of the shapes emerged from the black cloud. A single skeletal form draped in willowy robes of dark mist stroked Morningway's face before plunging its hand into his chest. Morningway convulsed and his eyes widened, his face contorting.

The soul eater withdrew its hand, holding a brilliant ball of light. It regarded the ball in its hand briefly before embracing Morningway. A hundred voices howled at once. The soul eater shredded the ball of light in its hand. The pieces fell away and turned to black smoke. The smoke wrapped tighter around them. The soul eater's shape melted into Morningway and spasms wracked his body. He thrashed and growled as his flesh began to tighten and rot.

Morningway's' limbs stretched and skin tore to reveal bone underneath. He fell against the altar as his face melted away. Finally, he threw his head back and his eyes erupted in bright flames which then died down into pale glowing points of light. The last wisps of black smoke shrank into the dragonfly pendant.

Morningway stood to his new height and flexed his changed body, stretching his face as he cackled. The other soul eaters became more agitated, thrashing against Katherine, Dorian, and Elisabeth. Morningway swung an arm over Elisabeth and drove the soul eaters from her. "Mine!"

There was no more time to wait. The soul eaters hadn't weakened or left; they were still pawing at Dorian and Katherine, taking small tastes of their life, increasing their appetite before they consumed them.

Katherine thought of Malcolm, and she forced her arm to move. She reached across the floor and took hold of her sword. Turning the tip of the blade down, she used it to prop herself up and then swung the gleaming blade through the air, scattering the soul eaters. They retreated, and this allowed Dorian to get back to his feet.

"Get Elisabeth out of here, Dorian," Katherine said. "I'll deal with Morningway."

They charged through the soul eaters, who lashed back at them with fierce claws. Each touch was a stab of ice, not enough to stop them but enough to slow their attack and weaken them. If they became too weak to fight, the soul eaters would finish them. Katherine drove one creature away from Dorian, slashing her sword through its wraith-like form. Dorian ducked under a swooping attack from another and caught it with a sweep of his axe. Though their attacks passed through the creatures, the force of each strike drove them back. Katherine leaped and vaulted over the altar, kicking Morningway against the wall.

Morningway hunched over and snarled at Katherine. He drew a saber from his belt and came at her with quick slashes. He wasn't as fast as her, however, and she was able to hold him off, deflecting each blow with her sword. She watched for an opening to strike back. The other soul eaters broke off from Katherine, swarming Dorian instead.

They soon threatened to overwhelm him, and Katherine had trouble making him out clearly through the roiling cloud. She heard a defiant cry and saw Dorian's axe dislodge one of the oil lamps. The lamp broke and spread burning oil over the floor.

A terrified howl pounded in Katherine's ears and she realized that the line of flame had cut her off from the exit. She was trapped with Morningway and Elisabeth.

"Dorian," Katherine cried, "you bloody fool!"

She felt the air shift as Morningway seized his chance. His saber struck her sword and ripped it from her hand, sending it through the flames. It clattered to the floor near Dorian. The soul eaters vanished one by one as the ritual components set on the summoning circle were destroyed by fire.

Morningway, his soul eater protected by its new earthly shell, swept his blade down once, cutting Katherine's wrist to the bone, then again, slashing open her stomach. He broke her jaw with an elbow to the face, and she crashed against some wood paneling on the wall behind her. She watched helplessly as Dorian scooped up her sword and fled, taking one last look at Elisabeth before he vanished.

Elisabeth cried, calling out Dorian's name. Morningway held his gnarled hand over her mouth. "Shh." More oil lamps cracked and ignited from the growing heat.

The wood behind Katherine's head gave way a little, revealing a hidden tunnel. It was a narrow opening and she had no idea where it led, but she would never make it through the fire and in her state she couldn't hope to defeat Morningway. It was the tunnel or oblivion.

Pushing her back against the panel, Katherine managed to break the wood enough to crawl backward into the tunnel. Morningway drew a glowing string of light from Elisabeth's mouth. He placed the glowing mass over the dragonfly pendant and clasped his hand around it. The light briefly filled the gold and emeralds of the pendant, then died. Morningway inhaled deeply and raised his fists in triumph.

"Mine. Mine forever!"

He turned his gaze to Katherine.

She crawled away as fast as she could. Each movement put pressure on her destroyed wrist and stretched her stomach wound, causing her to lose more and more blood. Worse still was the thick smoke flowing up the tunnel around her, blinding and choking her. Fear kept her moving.

She had failed Elisabeth. She cursed herself and prayed she would have the chance to make amends, to somehow find a way to restore Elisabeth's lost soul.

The pain was too much. Her lungs gave her no more air and her body was weak from lack of blood. She hoped she would die before Morningway reached her.

Before he took her, too.

But darkness was swift, and soon Katherine O'Reilly was gone.

Chapter Fourteen

NATHAN GASPED FOR AIR AND FELT HIS BODY FOR wounds. Morning had come at last and the dream was gone. The police let him make phone calls; he first called Ben to let him know he was okay and to wait at his house in case Laura came home. Then Nathan did what any young man in trouble would do. He called his father.

As Powell had promised, he'd been charged with trespassing, destruction of property, and disturbing the peace. As a result, Mike had to pay bail to have him released. If Powell found even the smallest bit of evidence that connected Nathan to the killings, he'd be after him like a hungry dog, so he cooperated as much as he was able, providing DNA and hair samples upon request, hoping it would dissuade Powell from pressing on with him as a primary suspect.

Mike arrived not long after being called, bringing Nathan a pair of black jeans, a black shirt, and an old pair of hiking boots.

"Couldn't find me a guitar to go with the Johnny Cash outfit?" Nathan said as he walked out of the station.

"It was all I had clean. Hope they fit."

"Yeah, they're fine. Thanks for coming to get me."

They took a cab to the parking garage where Nathan and Ben had left their cars. Most of the contents of Nathan's wallet had been ruined by the sewer muck, as had his cell phone. All he had left was his ATM card and credit card. Mike spoke to the attendant at the garage about the lost parking ticket and paid the fee. They drove to Mike's apartment in silence.

"I need to make a phone call," Nathan said. He went to the kitchen and lifted the receiver of the cream plastic phone hanging on the wall. He called Adams's cell phone.

It was Cadence who answered. "Nathan? We heard about what happened last night. Are you okay?"

"I'm fine. I've got information you might need. Where's Adams?"

"In a meeting with Dorian. Lane's with him. I'm in the hall, keeping my senses peeled."

"What's going on?"

"Negotiations. Our people are on their way in from Boston. They'll be arriving at Grand Central Station in less than an hour. The Council has agreed to allow us a chance to take down the soul eater, but they've left the finer details up to Dorian. They've been negotiating since before sunrise. Your little adventure last night drew a lot of attention."

"How did you find out about that?"

"Dorian's got agents everywhere, including the police. He's been oddly forthcoming with information. I don't trust him."

"Right there with you. Listen, I've remembered something. I was here before, in New York. I saw the soul eater."

"What happened?"

"It was summoned by a necromancer named Thaddeus Morningway. His wife was dying and he wanted to find some way to keep her soul from passing on, so he summoned a whole bunch of soul eaters and merged with one."

"Merged?"

"Like, they became one being." Nathan heard Cadence swear under her breath. "I guess that's bad," he said. "Huh?"

"Nathan, you're positive this is what happened?"

"It was a pretty vivid memory. I died."

"I've heard about wizards being able to bind demons and other entities to themselves like that, but I haven't seen it. And I've never heard of someone binding a soul eater to himself. Normally they're just given a fresh corpse to inhabit. Gods, this changes everything."

"How so?"

"Soul eaters are normally only partly corporeal and they need to wear someone down before they can consume them. Typically they stalk their prey for a few hours, taking small bites, invisibly, until the victim becomes tired and weary. After that they can feed properly. A soul eater given a living host body, one with that kind of magical power, would be able to consume a victim's soul in moments. And it would have true intelligence. Most soul eaters, even ones with physical bodies, are little more than animals."

"This sounds bad."

"It is, but it also gives us more options. When an otherworldly creature bonds itself to a mortal, both gain from each other's strengths, but they also have to share vulnerabilities and weaknesses. Morningway may have become a soul eater, but he's still going to be effected by magic, like mind control or mental compulsion."

"You can do that?"

"It's not easy, and it could be considered a violation of the Common Laws to control a person's mind, but Morningway isn't really human now. I might be able to whip up a few basic emotion spells, instill fear in him, urge him to be calm and non-violent, that sort of thing. But I'd need to be close to him. Unless you managed to get a sample of his hair or blood?"

"No, nothing like that. Listen, we need to regroup, and my cell phone's trashed. Call me at this number when Adams is out of his meeting and I'll head down to Grand Central to meet you."

"Got it. I have to go, I've got eavesdroppers. But Nathan, nice work."

Nathan thanked her and hung up. By the time he'd sat down at the kitchen table, his dad had already set down a mug of coffee.

"Strange conversation."

"Yeah."

"You want to tell me what's going on?"

"I wish I knew where to start. It's complicated and kinda crazy."

"I've seen a lot of weird things, son."

"Not like this. Everything is so messed up. I could be doing something really stupid."

"Why did you call me?"

"What?"

"There are obviously other people involved who can help you, who could've picked you up and bailed you out. I can understand you not wanting to get Laura mixed up in whatever this is, but I don't see what help I can be."

"I think I wanted your blessing."

Mike arched his eyebrows and leaned back in his chair.

"There are strange things happening," Nathan said. "Things that I wish I could stop believing in. Things I'm scared of. It's like I'm walking along the edge of a cliff, and if I take just one more step, I'll fall and I'll never be able to get back out."

Mike took a long breath and looked out the window for a moment. "Son, you're going to have a lot of times like this in your life, when what you want and what others need can't both happen. All that really matters then is what you believe is right."

"I have to give up everything to satisfy my conscience?"

"No, not quite. You have to figure out how you can help, while at the same time doing right by yourself and yours. These friends you're meeting at Grand Central, they can stop whatever's going on, right?"

Nathan nodded.

"And you can help them do it?"

"If they'll let me."

"Then how can you be the most help while making sure you don't lose everything you're trying to keep safe?"

Nathan finished his coffee. "You're not going to ask me what's really going on, are you?"

Mike shrugged, but the phone rang before he could answer. Nathan grabbed it quickly. It was Cadence.

"We're on," she said. "Grand Central, thirty minutes." She hung up.

"I have to go," Nathan said.

"I'm coming with you."

"Dad, this could be dangerous."

"I know when to stay out of the way. Besides, you're a possible suspect in a murder investigation. If something happens, you'll need a reliable witness to testify in your defense."

"I can't ask you to do that."

"You're not asking and I'm not offering. Now do as your father tells you and get me my coat."

Nathan and his dad drove to Grand Central station together, but Mike offered to stay with the car and keep the parking meter fed. Nathan was quietly relieved.

The morning's commuters had long since passed through the terminal's stalls. Nathan gave only passing concern to the fact he was supposed to be at work and once again hadn't called his boss to let him know he wouldn't be in.

Grand Central Station was an incredible example of quality New York architecture, like the Department of Records where Nathan worked. He had often come here to appreciate the craftsmanship in the high marble walls and the figures from Greek mythology painted on the ceiling, especially when the sun would stream in through the arched windows high up at the top of the concourse.

Adams was waiting for Nathan at the foot of the stairs leading down from the entrance. With him were Cadence and Lane, along with six men carrying large duffle bags. They eyed Nathan suspiciously as he walked down to meet them. He nodded to them. The terminal wasn't exceptionally busy, but even so, Grand Central was never free of people.

"Not exactly the most private place to meet," Nathan said.

"You'd be amazed what people will ignore," Adams said, "and it guarantees us some measure of protection in case any of Dorian's goons didn't get the memo about us being here. These are some friends from Boston. They're here to help with our little infestation problem."

Names were exchanged, though Adams's friends weren't exactly the warmest bunch. Nathan glanced at Cadence and she gave an encouraging nod.

"I've got information," he said.

Adams folded his arms. "I know, Cadence told us. You found its nest?"

"It's under a building site near Murray Street. I think Dorian was looking for it. It was his construction company that was carrying out the work. Seems like too much of a coincidence that just before it was due to wake up again, workers began clearing the way for new foundations to be poured."

"Murdoch and Sullivan owns a lot of construction companies," Lane said. "It's not unreasonable that it was chance."

Nathan shook his head. "No, Dorian knows what's under there. He was with me when Morningway changed."

Adams raised an eyebrow, and Nathan saw the beginning of a smirk.

"Dorian came to me for help, when I was Katherine O'Reilly. It was his job to handle Morningway, but he wasn't strong enough on his own. And I think Dorian was in love with Morningway's wife."

"Makes sense he'd be eager to help us," Cadence said, "if he wants revenge on Morningway."

"Agreed," Adams said. "We should be cautious at the meeting."

"What meeting?" asked Nathan.

"After Cadence told me what you'd remembered I was able to go back to Dorian with a request to hunt in Morningway's nest. Naturally he didn't want us crawling through the whole city causing trouble. Dorian agreed, on the condition that his own men go along."

"Who?"

"Eli and Gideon along with some revenants."

Revenants. Katherine's memories of them were strong. Walking corpses. The Council of Chains granted low-ranking mortal agents a form of immortality by ritually trapping their souls in their bodies after death. Though resistant to pain and never tiring, they could be killed by cutting off their heads.

"Does the Council think that's necessary? You've got a small army here. That's got to be enough to kill Morningway, right?"

"Because the vampires and revenants aren't there to kill Morningway," Adams said. "They're to make sure we don't double-cross Dorian."

"Why would Dorian be worried about that? You're going to kill the soul eater."

"Morningway's not like a normal soul eater," Adams said. "He's got a lot of power, and he's intelligent. Trying to destroy him in a straight fight is a bad idea. But Cadence found a spell which might tip the odds in our favor."

Cadence swore under her breath and walked away from the group.

"The strength of a soul eater lies in its phylactery," Adams continued. "If you destroy it, the soul eater dies. My theory is that Morningway's got his own phylactery, and if we can get it, we can use a spell to control him."

The dragonfly pendant. Morningway had drawn the essence of both his wife and the soul eater he merged with into the pendant. It had to be his phylactery.

"Control him? But you wanted to destroy him!" Nathan looked over at Cadence. Of course. "You want him as a weapon, don't you?"

"It's something to consider. As well as trying to find a way to draw on the knowledge of the souls he's got trapped, imagine what we could do with a creature that none of the Council could oppose. We could take back New York, then move on to other places, wiping out the Council wherever we found it."

"But you said the soul eater was an abomination."

"Fuck abomination, I've got a shot at winning a war we thought we'd lost years ago. Now tell me what Morningway's phylactery looks like."

Nathan backed away. "No, no way. I'm through. I'm out."

"You're never out."

"You never wanted me involved in the first place." Nathan started walking up the stairs. "You get your wish. You're on your own."

"No, Nathan," Adams said, "you are."

Nathan heard quick footsteps on the marble stairs. Cadence called his name.

"What?" he replied.

"I'm sorry," she said. "Adams was never going to just kill Morningway, not when he has a chance to control him instead. I know that now."

"Why are you helping him do it?"

"Adams may be an asshole but he's got some clout back home. If I turn my back on him, I could be in for some trouble. And I figure, if I'm the one controlling Morningway, at least I can make sure he's not used to hurt anyone. Maybe I can convince the Conclave to force Adams to destroy him."

"What about all those people Morningway took? What about Miranda? Lane cared about her, didn't he? Does he get a say in what happens to her soul?"

"Gods, Nathan, this isn't easy for me. All my life I've been raised to follow the Common Laws and protect the sanctity of life and death. This goes against everything I believe, but I'm not in a position to make demands. I'm sorry." She looked away. "We never came here to save New

York, Nathan. We came to do a job, then go home. We can't do any more."

"Because of the treaty."

"Not just that. Every place has energy, an essence of its own, like people do. If you pay attention, open your senses to the world around you, you'll feel it. New York is … heavy. Like it's wrapped in chains. Do you know how much strength it takes to change that? To stand up and fight that energy with such force that the city itself, and everyone in it, feels the difference?"

"I guess not."

"More strength than I have and a damn sight more determination than Adams could ever muster. He wants the easiest way to get the job done, at any cost. If others are lost on the way, he could care less. That's not the kind of force that can help this city. We're nobody's heroes. We're just the last dregs of a long-beaten army."

Nathan shook his head.

"Please, Nathan." Cadence reached for his arm and squeezed it gently. "If I don't know what I'm looking for, we'll have to fight him. Sure, we might end up killing him, but there's also a damn good chance he'll get some of us first."

"Maybe you should have thought about that before showing up where you don't belong."

Cadence lowered her hand. "Fine." She walked away.

Nathan quickly turned and left the station.

Chapter Fifteen

NATHAN DIDN'T SAY MUCH AS HE DROVE AWAY from the station. After he had circled the same block for the fifth time, Mike finally spoke.

"Are you hungry?" he asked. "Because I'm starved."

"What do you feel like?"

"Chinese. There's a place just down here." He pointed to a turn up ahead.

At the restaurant, Nathan picked up a selection of spring rolls, noodles, and other items, as well as two bottles of Coke. He paid the parking meter up for the next hour so he and Mike could sit and eat in the car. His head hurt.

"Have I just made a big mistake?" he asked his dad.

"No," Mike said, "satay is fine. I like spicy."

Nathan tucked into the noodles with a pair of cheap chopsticks. "I think I just walked away."

"What's next?"

"Home, I guess." Nathan washed down his noodles with some Coke and slouched in the car seat. "It's getting late. Laura will be worried, and I need to check in with Ben."

Like Cadence said, she and her team hadn't come here looking to save New York. They didn't care a damn about what happened here, so long as they got what they came for.

Nathan hoped that if he were in their position, where he could make a difference, he wouldn't let some old treaty or bullshit about not being strong enough to change things get in his way. He'd make a stand.

And for a moment Nathan almost believed himself. The truth was, he was relieved, glad he'd walked away. Now he could put it all behind him and start living again. He could have what Katherine had wanted. That was fair, right? It seemed like he'd known nothing lately but strange murders, dark alleys, and hidden secrets. It would be nice to go back to worrying about groceries and mortgage payments. Maybe the dreams would stop.

"Hey," Nathan said, "you wanna come over? Laura would love to see you. And I think I could do with the back-up when I apologize to her."

"Sure, son."

It was almost dark when Nathan managed to fight his way through rush hour traffic to get home. Dim light came through the windows. Laura was home. Ben's car was in the driveway.

He got out of the car, pausing to take the small black box from the glove compartment. It felt good to finally have this in his hand. He went inside, his dad close behind him. Laura was sitting on the couch next to Ben, with just a table lamp providing light.

"Nathan!" She got up and approached him. "Where have you been? Your office called, said you didn't show up for work today and they couldn't reach you. Then Ben came over saying something about exploring some basement sewer and some monster that was chasing you. What's going on?"

"I was in jail," he said.

"Jail?" She reached back as if to slap him, but pulled back when Nathan held up his hands.

"What was it this time," she said, "more trespassing? Did you get in a fight?" She turned and leaned on the back of the couch, slowing her breathing. "You know what? I don't want to know. Whatever you've been doing with Cynthia, whatever the hell you've gotten yourself involved in, it's too much."

"It is," he said. "All of it. And it's okay. I'm through with it. I'm out, and I want to do things right."

Taking a deep breath, Nathan knelt on one knee and held up the small box. His heart raced and he felt glad to have Ben and his father there.

Laura's eyes fell to the black box. She bit her lip. "What's that?"

"Laura." Nathan's mouth was suddenly dry. "You're the world to me."

"Stop," she said.

"I'm sorry for all of the things I've done wrong, and I promise you I'll do better."

"Nathan, please just stop."

"Laura, will you marry me?"

"Damn it, Nathan." Laura clenched her hands together. "I'm pregnant."

He leaped up to hug her, lifting her off the floor. "That's fantastic!" He swung her around and set her back down again. "We can get married and have the baby and…"

She wasn't smiling. Her lip trembled, and she blinked away tears.

"What's wrong?"

She took an uneasy breath before speaking. "It's not yours, Nathan."

He didn't say anything right away. He stepped away from Laura. A sick feeling grew in his stomach; he wanted to run out the door or punch the wall or break something. Thinking back over the last several days, he saw the pieces come together. He finally understood what had been happening. It didn't make him feel any better, but it gave him something to focus on instead of the pit of bile heaving in his stomach, like biting down on a finger to distract from an injured leg.

"It's too soon, of course," he said slowly. "We hadn't made love for months before a few nights ago. You'd never have known you were pregnant so soon."

He tried to keep his voice steady. He had to know more. Now that he knew the worst, not knowing the rest would kill him. "How long?"

"Nathan—"

"How long?" he repeated, a little harder than before.

"About six weeks."

Nathan took long breaths to stay calm. "You planned to lie to me, weren't you? That's why you slept with me that night. So you could say the baby was mine and I'd have no reason to doubt."

Laura nodded a little. "I couldn't in the end. I can't bring a child into this, Nathan. It's not fair."

"No. Of course not," Nathan said.

He studied Ben's face. Ben turned away to stare at the floor, then his gaze flicked to Laura.

Nathan remembered all the times Ben had been there to counsel him on his relationship, how he'd acted as a go-between when Laura wasn't speaking to him. How he'd warned her he was going to lose her. Nathan's expression hardened. It all made sense.

"How long have you two been seeing each other?"

Laura and Ben exchanged glances. "About a year now," she said.

"A year," Nathan said. "And you never said anything."

"Would you have listened?" Laura jerked her face up and advanced. "Once you and Cynthia started spending so much time together, you changed. You spent so little time at home, with me. What was I supposed to think? It's not even like I meant anything to happen. It was an accident. You were cold and you stopped talking to me. All I wanted was someone to touch me again!"

She slapped Nathan across the face. It stung and her nails scraped him. He blinked and stayed silent.

"You were never a real man," she said, "not what I needed."

She circled Nathan. "These bruises you were so worried about?" She rolled back her sleeves. "When Ben fucks me, he holds me down. He's rough, strong. And you know what? I like it."

Nathan's skin prickled. He glanced back at his dad, aware that he'd be hearing this. Nathan's face flushed.

"You were so god-damned self absorbed you couldn't see what was happening right under your nose. What does that make you?"

"A better man than you deserve." His face cooled and his shoulders settled. He was done. "Excuse me."

He walked past her, ignoring her swearing and shouting. He went to their room where he packed a few things into a small overnight bag and slung it over his shoulder. He went into the garage and put his rattan sticks, the three foot lengths of wood used in his escrima classes, into their carrying case and slung that over his other shoulder before grabbing his toolbox and going back inside. He didn't look at Laura, but she tried to get in his way and make him listen to her.

"Are you just going to avoid me now?" she shouted as Nathan handed the toolbox to his father. Mike left the room, taking the box out to the car.

"Nathan," Laura said. "Are you even listening?"

Nathan's heart pounded. "A week ago, something like this would have killed me. Right now I've got more important things to worry about. I tried to be the man I thought you wanted. I know I wasn't. I got things wrong and I'm sorry, but there's something out there that's killing people and now the people who can stop it need my help, so if you don't mind, I'm going to deal with that first."

"You don't even care."

"Of course I care." Nathan swallowed back spit. "I love you. I wanted to be with you, and I screwed it up. You'll never know how sorry I am for that." He looked from Laura to Ben. "And for what you felt you had to do."

He stepped closer to Ben. "But you. You're supposed to be my friend. I trusted you." Nathan pointed at Laura. "She trusted you, and you take advantage of her like this?"

"It's not like that," Ben said. "I love her."

Nathan shut his eyes and turned away. "You should have just left me, Laura. I can't believe the two of you would do this."

"I'm sorry, Nathan," Ben said. "You…"

"I know. I'm like a brother to you." Nathan walked out and slammed the door behind him.

He and Mike got into the car and drove away, back toward Manhattan.

"Guess I really messed everything up," Nathan said as they neared the Queensboro Bridge.

"People make mistakes."

"She was having an affair with my best friend."

Mike shrugged.

"How did I not see it? There had to have been signs. That's what I do. I see signs, connect the pieces. This was right in front of me."

"Those can be the hardest things to see, especially if you don't have any reason to think something's wrong."

"I was what was wrong."

"Laura and Ben made their own choices."

"Son of a bitch took advantage of her. What kind of a person am I to let that happen?"

Mike reached across and squeezed Nathan's arm. "You're my son."

"You're not disappointed in me for messing things up?"

"There are a lot of things that make up a man. Whatever you did wrong, Laura's choices were her own. You live, you learn, you try to do better."

Nathan nodded and kept driving. He replayed events in his mind; all the times when he might have been able to save his relationship, all the things he'd given up because he thought it might help. He hadn't wanted to take the job in the Department of Records. He'd wanted to keep studying, for a while at least. Maybe get himself a PhD, maybe teach history. But he and Laura needed two incomes to afford a decent house, and they had talked about having a family. He couldn't expect her to support him while he was in school.

After all, that wouldn't have been fair.

Nathan looked out the window at the Manhattan skyline. The sun had long since set and the city was lit by a thousand bright lights glowing in the distance.

The plan had been to let Adams take on Morningway. The plan had been to find information, pass it on, and let the other reborn save the day and then hope they stuck around to take on Dorian and the other things eating away at the soul of the city. Nathan frowned and stared at the road ahead. The plan had been shot to hell.

They crossed onto the Queensboro Bridge. "I made a choice earlier," Nathan said. "To walk away. The people I thought were going to help … they're not. The guy in charge just wants to get something for himself and then leave. They're not staying."

"I don't pretend to understand everything that's going on with you," Mike said, "but can you really blame them?"

Nathan glanced at Mike, his eyebrows raised.

"Think about it. They have their own homes to look to, their own loved ones to protect. Can you really expect them to abandon all that?"

"I've lost Laura," Nathan said. "Ben, too. Cynthia's in the hospital. The police think I'm a murderer. What do I have to look to?"

"You've always got New York," Mike said with a smile. "And your old man." He gave Nathan a pat on the shoulder. "All the choices you've made have brought you to this. They've made you into a man who can't let people get hurt. A man who'll do something about it even if it seems like a bad decision, or he suffers because of it. I couldn't be prouder to call you my son."

Before Nathan could respond, a car rammed into them.

It struck from Nathan's side, blindsiding him. He felt his head jerk to one side. He held on tight to the steering wheel as his car swerved. The other car slammed into him again. Nathan saw the rough shape of it as it shoved his car across the road. It was big; big enough to completely overpower his four-door sedan.

Mike watched the car, hands gripping the passenger door and his seat.

"Hold on!" Nathan shouted.

They crashed through the barrier along the side of the bridge. Nathan's seatbelt snapped tight against his chest.

The car jolted and water rushed around them as they were surrounded by darkness. Water bubbled into the car, swirling around Nathan's legs. Mike's head was bleeding. He unbuckled his seat belt and turned on the interior light.

"Get your belt off," Mike said as he climbed into the back seat.

Nathan could feel them continue to sink. He breathed slowly to try and control his racing heartbeat.

Mike pulled him into the back seat and shoved the rattan sticks and overnight bag into his hands. "Here." He took a claw hammer from the toolbox. "Take a deep breath and get ready to swim."

He nodded and inhaled deeply. Mike hit the rear window with the clawed end of the hammer. The glass broke after three strikes and water came rushing in. The water pushed Nathan back, but Mike grabbed his hand and steadied him.

The car quickly filled with water. It was freezing, despite the August heat. Mike climbed out of the sinking vehicle, pulling Nathan up with him. The swim was hard on Nathan, fighting through the cold. The two breached the water's surface, gasping for air.

Someone pulled him out of the water and dropped him onto the deck of a motorboat. Mike fell next to him. A familiar, fanged face sneered at them. Eli.

Eli barked an order and the boat's engine powered up, taking them toward Manhattan.

"Saved us the trouble of coming down after you," he said. The vampire drew a gun and aimed it at Mike. "Behave yourselves, and this'll all be over nice and easy."

Nathan still felt disoriented from the fall. His arms and legs ached from the swim to the surface.

The boat took them to a small pier on the southeast side of Manhattan where Eli ordered them off. He tucked the gun away. Another pair of vampires stood guard behind Nathan and Mike.

Two cars sat in a small parking lot at the top of the pier. One was a large 4x4 with a dent in the front, probably the one that had run them off the road. The other was a dark red sports car. Gideon stepped out of the 4x4.

"Friends?" Mike asked.

"Oh yeah," Nathan said. "We go way back."

Eli smiled. "You ought to tell Ms. Brooke to be more careful about where she uses her cell phone. And you were right," he flashed his teeth. "Grand Central Station is a terrible place to tell your boss your little secrets, Ms. O'Reilly."

Nathan inhaled sharply.

Eli stood nose to nose with Nathan. "If you've got Katherine O'Reilly's memories in your head that means you know about Morningway's talisman. Tell me what it is."

"What's going on, Nathan?" Mike asked.

"They want information," Nathan said, "to control the thing that's been killing people." He met Eli's stare. "That's the plan, isn't it? Beat Adams to the punch, use a ritual to take control of the soul eater for Dorian?"

"Ritual, blackmail, threats of oblivion, there are so many options. Do you know what the phylactery looks like?"

"Not a chance. I'm not going to help give Dorian a weapon like that."

"Even if it's to save the soul of the woman he loves?" Eli asked. "I thought you'd be a bit more sympathetic than that."

"You must think I was reborn yesterday if you think I'll believe that's all Dorian wants."

Eli chuckled. "A joke, I like that. Unfortunately I don't have time to swap laughs."

The vampires standing behind Nathan and Mike pulled their arms behind their backs. Nathan struggled, but the vampire twisted his arms, wrenching the shoulder joints. Eli stepped in closer to Nathan and pushed his head to one side before leaning in.

The pain was cold at first. Eli's teeth punctured the flesh between Nathan's neck and shoulder. Searing heat followed as Eli bit down. Nathan screamed and jerked, trying to pull free. His vision blurred, and he felt his muscles seize.

Nathan convulsed, unable to think or breathe as Eli fed from him. Finally the seizure abated; his muscles relaxed and became weak. He felt pressure on his neck, like getting an injection. The vampires released him and he collapsed onto the pier, trembling as the world spun in circles. He touched the bite wound. His hand came back bloody, but it didn't feel that bad. The pain was already fading.

Eli drew a long knife from a sheath on his belt. "Now, Shepherd," he said, "you're going to tell me what I need to know, aren't you?"

Nathan's head flopped without him wanting it to, nodding yes. *What? No* … "I … you hurt Cynthia…"

Speaking made him feel sick. Moving was too hard. Doing as Eli asked was much easier.

"I'll kill others if you don't cooperate. You wouldn't want that, would you?"

"No." The words slipped form Nathan's lips. Something was wrong. Why couldn't he move? Why was the nice man he trusted holding a knife?

No. Eli was a vampire, an agent of Dorian. Nathan felt the ache in his neck, where he'd been bitten, and remembered how Adams had checked him for bite marks. How the girl in the alley had been unwilling to run from the vampire who had attacked her. The bite must have done something to him. He had to stay quiet.

"Please don't." Nathan fought to keep from speaking, but the words kept coming. "Laura's pregnant. Don't hurt the baby. My dad, let him go. Let him go."

"Nathan," Eli said with a sing-song voice. "Tell me what Morningway's phylactery looks like. That's all I want."

Nathan didn't dare to look at Eli. *Say nothing.* His mouth moved so he bit down on his tongue. Blood trickled down his throat.

"I'll count to three," Eli said. "And then I'll kill your father."

Nathan looked up and saw that Eli had his knife pressed against Mike's throat. "No!"

"One."

"Don't tell him anything," Mike said, eyes fixed forward.

"Two." Eli pressed the blade in more. Though it drew a tiny drop of blood, Mike didn't flinch.

"Stop!" Nathan flailed at Eli's legs with limp arms. "It's a dragonfly," he said. "It's a pendant shaped like a dragonfly."

Eli withdrew the knife. Nathan lay on the ground, his lungs heaving.

"Just a pendant?" Eli asked.

"It belonged to his wife. Morningway took it and used it as the focus for his ritual. The soul eater's essence is inside."

"Thank you, Nathan."

Eli impaled Mike on his knife. Mike coughed and blood dribbled from his lips. He staggered, but the vampire behind him held him up. Eli pulled the blade out, spraying the deck with blood.

Eli licked the knife clean, shivering briefly. "Mmm, strong." He dropped the knife on the deck.

So close to Nathan, and he still couldn't bring himself to reach for it.

"When the old man is dead, toss him into the river. Keep the kid. We can have fun with him later."

"You lied," Nathan said. He tried to crawl after Eli, but his body was too heavy. He could barely hold up his head.

"Of course I lied." Eli joined Gideon and the pair left in the sports car. The remaining vampires started to laugh.

"Nathan," Mike said. "Gotta get up."

Nathan slumped forward and looked up at his father. One of the vampires guarding him stuck his finger into Mike's wound and licked the blood from it. Mike grunted in pain.

Nathan tried to speak. He wanted to act, to say he was sorry, that now they were both going to die because of him.

But he could only watch Mike's face.

He saw Mike lift his head to meet the eyes of the vampire before him. He saw Mike's old, scarred hands curl into fists.

The laughter stopped.

Mike broke the nose of the vampire holding him with the back of his head. He pulled free. Hands which had broken down doors, climbed buildings, and carried the injured, pummeled the other vampire. A blow to the abdomen made him double over and drop the knife. Two balled-up fists to the back sent it to the ground long enough for Mike to pull a splintered plank of wood from the pier.

He snapped part of the plank across the face of the doubled-over vampire, knocking it into the river. The one with the broken nose got back on his feet. Mike lunged, holding the broken, pointed piece of wood out ahead of him. They fell onto the pier in a heap, Mike gasping for breath and the vampire gasping in pain.

The wood had gone through the vampire's chest. The vampire convulsed and tried to claw at him while its flesh began to crack and burn. Smoke rose from broken skin and the body stiffened, turning gray, before it fell apart into a cloud of ash.

The second vampire climbed up from the river. Mike quickly grabbed the knife lying on the deck and raked it in a wide arc. He tore through most of the neck. Its head flopped to the side. Mike kicked the head, ripping the last of its flesh free. The body fell and sank back into the water below the pier, while the head landed with a splash several feet away.

Nathan felt Mike's arms around him, lifting him up. His dad was having trouble breathing, and he moved slowly. Still, he carried Nathan over his shoulder, down the pier.

Mike placed him in the passenger seat of the 4x4 and buckled him in before climbing into the driver's seat. The keys had been left in the ignition. He started the engine. Nathan heard his voice as he drove.

"Nathan. Can you hear me?" It was the fifth time Mike had tried to get a response from him. Or the sixth? "Tell me where to go."

"Hos … hospital…" Nathan tried to say. Mike needed a doctor, and fast.

"No, son," he said. "You got bitten. There's something wrong with you, and you need help. Tell me where to go."

Nathan tried to shake his head, but only managed to make it fall to one side. "Hospital…"

"Listen to me," Mike said. "Whatever happens, you have to pull through, got it? I'll be okay, but doctors can't fix what's happened to you, now tell me where we can find whoever can."

"Park," he murmured, without thinking. "Riverside Park. Roland … find Roland…"

Time passed in a haze. Nathan was aware of Mike assuring him that everything would be okay, repeating words of comfort as they weaved through the streets.

They stopped. Mike took him from the car, holding him up. There was a house up ahead, and the door was open, but they weren't going that way. Nathan felt another body next to him and realized that Roland was under his left arm, helping Mike carry him.

"Sanctuary," he managed to say.

"Yeah, yeah," Roland grumbled.

They brought Nathan down into Freedom Tunnel. He only barely registered the people staring as he went by. Something fell to the floor and there was shouting. Faces blurred into one another. He couldn't tell who was who.

Eventually someone set Nathan down in a wooden chair. He watched as a young, pretty woman with ash-blonde hair removed his shirt, and for a moment he thought he'd drifted off into some kind of dream.

Cold water hit his face, the shock bringing him to his senses.

He was in a chair in The Lost's cave. Libby watched from a short distance away, her face stern and unreadable. The young woman to his right wore a plain brown dress that fell to her ankles.

On his left, a large man with dark skin fastened a leather restraint around his wrist, securing it to the arm of the chair. Nathan felt a sudden surge of panic. Roland stepped into view and fastened Nathan's right arm. His ankles had already been secured.

"What's happening?" The words came out slurred.

Roland nodded to the young woman.

"My name is Danielle," she said. "I'll try not to make this hurt."

"What?"

Danielle went to an old table where she dipped a small clay jug into a large ceramic bowl. She returned and emptied the jug slowly over the bite wound on Nathan's neck.

The liquid was cold, but the wound burned and he heard a sizzling sound. The pain drove down into his body through the open wound, every beat of his heart pulling the sensation deeper into him, until his body was suffused with an intense heat. He gritted his teeth and managed not to cry out.

The experience ended shortly after the jug emptied and he took long, deep breaths to steady himself. Already he could feel his senses returning to normal.

"Ow. What was that?"

"A mixture to burn out the infection from the bite," Danielle said.

"What? Holy water? I tired that on a vampire before; it did nothing."

Roland laughed from a corner. "No, not holy water. It's a special potion we brew up to get that crap out of your system quickly."

Nathan nodded and looked up at Danielle. "Thank you."

She smiled briefly. "Don't thank me yet. There's one more thing."

Nathan frowned as the dark-skinned man walked over to a fireplace set into a stone alcove and kneeled down, rustling the hot coals with a poker. It glowed bright orange.

"Be gentle, Kian," Danielle said. She turned and left the room.

Libby stepped in and shut the battered old door behind her. She stood next to Roland and watched.

"What's going on?" Nathan asked. "What's he going to do, Roland?"

"Sorry, kid. The potion purges the venom, but if that wound's not cleaned up properly, those vampires will smell you a mile away."

"Cleaned up?" Nathan struggled against the restraints. "Roland, you son of a bitch, let me go!"

"Not up to me." Roland tipped his head to Libby. "This is her decision. Now stop being a baby."

Nathan watched Kian with the glowing poker in his hand. He gave an understanding nod before tilting his head to one side and shutting his eyes.

Kian pressed the red-hot poker down onto Nathan's flesh, holding it on the wound from Eli's bite. The pain was excruciating. He clenched his hands and jaw shut.

His dad had once told him what it was like to be burned. The sudden numbness. The cold feeling just as the realization of what happened struck home. Then the long, constant pain. And the smell. This was everything Mike had described, and worse.

Despite himself, he screamed.

When he woke up some time later, Nathan realized he had been moved. He lay on a soft mattress under a blanket in a small chamber. His clothes hung near a fireplace to dry. The heat from the fire was comforting, but it made his neck twinge. He reached for the wound, sending a ripple of pain as the burned flesh stretched.

The wound had been treated with a clean dressing, held in place by bandages around his neck and chest. Antiseptic fumes wafted up from the dressing. He sat up and dressed himself, finding the task difficult due to the pain and lingering weakness in his limbs.

Then he remembered.

Dad.

He laced up his boots and hurried out of the bedchamber.

Chapter Sixteen

CADENCE LOOKED AROUND THE CONSTRUCTION site and shivered. They'd been waiting an hour for Dorian's people to show. The walled-in construction site offered a lot of privacy, so they could freely carry their weapons and other equipment without drawing attention.

Adams held a tactical shotgun, one of those ones with a folding shoulder stock and pistol grip. He wore Kevlar under his jacket as well as two back-up pistols and a knife.

Lane wore a handgun on his hip and carried a curved axe with a four-foot wooden haft, the end of which had been sharpened into a point. They both had a lot of combat experience between them and it showed in their casual manner.

The men Adams had brought in from Boston looked more apprehensive. Two were armed with shotguns similar to Adams's, while three had handguns and short staffs. They watched the shadows and checked their weapons. The sixth had climbed up into the neck of a crane on the site, where he monitored the site entrance through the scope of a silenced sniper rifle.

Adams was nothing if not prepared.

Standing among these guys with a bag of spell ingredients over her shoulder and a gnarled wooden staff she used to help focus the energies for her magic, Cadence felt outclassed. Of course, none of the others had the magical ability needed to hold Morningway long enough to subdue him. If he was as powerful as a normal soul eater, bullets and blades wouldn't be much use against him.

Cadence had marked out a pentacle around the hole in the ground where Nathan had found Morningway's lair. Salt was an effective barrier against malevolent spirits, when it was used correctly, and she had marked the five points of the star with stubby candles, now burning away. The salt represented earth, while the burning candles and the wisps of smoke they produced called on fire and air, respectively.

She anointed the center of the pentacle with three drops from a bottle of mineral water. Rituals were best done either drawing on the full power of all the elements or with specific sigils and runes crafted in accordance with age-old traditions of spellcraft. There wasn't time to lay down the right symbols for the spell. This would have to do.

This would have been easier if Nathan had told them what Morningway's phylactery looked like. If it could be wrestled away from Morningway, Cadence would whip up a mind control spell on will alone. Morningway might listen to reason if his phylactery was in danger.

Cadence looked over her shoulder at the sound of crunching gravel. Eli and Gideon led over a dozen men in overalls through the site's gate. As they came closer, she saw that their flesh was grey and rotten, missing entirely in some places. Revenants. Though they looked like nothing more than animated corpses, their minds brimmed with human intelligence and cunning.

Cadence wasn't used to seeing so many of them outdoors and above ground. The gentle pulse of magical energy suggested they were being masked by a weak glamour—an illusion designed to make people overlook their horrific appearance. The spell played on expectations. Mundanes never think they are going to see a rotting corpse walking down the street, so their minds block the image, changing it into something more acceptable. It was easy to perform and lasted a long time, but anyone aware of the existence of the supernatural would see through it easily enough.

Eli and Gideon wore matching suits; blue pinstripe, fitted perfectly. Eli stepped forward to shake Adams's hand. Cadence eyed the swords belted around their waists, and the bulge under the left arm of each, indicating concealed handguns.

"You came prepared," Adams said.

"Dorian wanted to make sure your people were well protected." Eli flashed his fangs.

"Let's just get this done," Adams said. He stepped back around the pentacle, always facing Eli, and gave a nod to Cadence.

Cadence knelt before the circle. She held her staff in both hands and raised it. Through it, she drew essence, the building block of all things material and immaterial.

It flowed from within her and spread like a wave toward the pentacle.

"Thaddeus Morningway, Thaddeus Morningway, Thaddeus Morningway," she chanted. "We call to you, who have breached the veil between life and death, become the thing which feeds on life yet does not live. By my power I summon thee. By my power I bind thee. So may it be, so may it be."

Cadence felt a surge of power as her own essence reached out under the ground and then suddenly pulled back. There was resistance, like reeling in a big fish on a line; she decided to release a larger amount of energy into the ritual as she said the third and final incantation.

"So may it be!"

There was no flash of light or crack of thunder. Cadence felt as though her lungs had just filled with fire, but the others watching only heard the whoosh of wind and a dreadful howl from the chambers below.

The soul eater shot up from the hole. Adams, Lane, and the reborn backed away and covered their eyes as dirt flew at them. Eli and Gideon flinched. The revenants remained still.

Cadence held her concentration, keeping her eyes locked on the soul eater as she channeled her energy around it.

The soul eater snapped back to the ground, landing in the middle of the ritual circle. The force cracked the stone. Morningway struggled but couldn't break free. Cadence realized she had been over-zealous. Still, it was no harm to have overkill on a creature like this.

As long as she maintained her concentration and a steady flow of energy, the spell would hold. She just needed time to deepen the control. Speaking the incantation to control Morningway's mind gave her a hollow feeling. Though he was a hideous monster now, he had once been human, and doing such a thing to a human mind went against everything she had been taught about magic.

Cadence pressed her will against his and he pressed right back, proving he hadn't lost the magical talent he'd gained in life. Nathan had said Morningway could control even the necromantic energies that infused the bodies of undead creatures.

Cadence didn't dare look away, but Morningway's sneer told her he saw the fear in her eyes. If she stopped chanting, the spell would break and he would be loose. If that happened, Morningway would take control of Eli, Gideon, and their revenants.

Cadence tried to remain calm. She had time, after all. She was well-rested, and she could draw on surrounding energy from the environment. If no one physically broke her circle, she could maintain it with ease and break down Morningway's mental defenses.

Eli stepped closer to the imprisoned soul eater.

"Something's wrong," she heard Jim say.

"Give her time," Adams said. He was watching Morningway, not paying attention to Eli, who was right up against the ritual circle.

Eli lunged forward. Cadence held her breath.

There was a *thwip* sound as Adam's sniper took a shot, but it was too late. The bullet just split Eli's jacket across the shoulder.

Eli's feet scrubbed the line of the circle. This let the magical energy disperse safely, without lashing back at him.

Cadence wasn't so lucky. She felt a rush of power as her spell collapsed. The force threw her onto her back and she hit her head. Her vision blurred while she pressed her hands to the ground and channeled the spell's energy back into the earth before it caused more damage.

Even with the grounding, the shock had left her weakened. The struggle to control Morningway and break into his mind had been draining. The backlash left her whole body numb and limp. She heard gunshots and sounds of fighting. She lifted her head as Eli pulled something away from the soul eater. It shimmered briefly and he held it up. A pendant. A dragonfly.

"Thaddeus Morningway," Eli called, "by my blood and by your bond I command you to submit, obey and serve me, Eli Vance of the Council of Chains!"

He made a motion with his left hand, and Cadence felt essence flow to Eli. He bit into his palm and pressed it to the gold pendant.

Bastard! That was her spell. The first spell she'd researched to control Morningway, the one that relied on getting hold of his phylactery. Eli had found out about it, but how? She felt her essence being pulled away from the remains of the circle. Eli had stolen some of Cadence's energy to fuel the spell. She cursed herself as she fought for her body to work again.

The soul eater turned on the reborn, leading the revenants in a charge. Adams and Lane were shouting. Though her limbs hurt as the feeling came back into them, Cadence dragged herself along the ground toward the voices, praying to all the gods she knew that they'd find a way out of this.

Nathan found Roland in a common room near Libby's chambers. It was large enough for a sizeable group to sit comfortably in the salvaged armchairs and sofas, but right now it was empty but for Nathan, Roland, and Libby.

"Roland, look, about what happened."

"We know, kid." He eased Nathan onto a couch and checked his bandages. "Your dad told us everything," he said, keeping his gaze down. "Hell of a guy."

"Is he okay?"

Roland lit a cigarette. "We called an ambulance when you arrived and they took him to the hospital. But we don't know, really."

Nathan watched Roland's expression shift. He wasn't giving him the whole story. "You must have seen a lot of injuries," he said. "Both of you."

He looked across at Libby, who was seated in a comfortable-looking easy chair, fiddling with a pair of knitting needles and a ball of blue wool. "And the paramedics must have said something, right?"

Libby and Roland exchanged a long glance. "It's not good," Roland said. "The wound was bad, and he lost a lot of blood getting you here. He was barely hanging on when they arrived. I'm sorry."

"It's my fault," Nathan said. "If I'd done something—been stronger—he'd be okay. Damn it, Roland, he just wanted to open a bar. This isn't how it was meant to be."

"Not everything goes according to plan," Roland said. "Besides which, you must have gained something, right? Got something to show for it all?"

Nathan snarled at Roland. "A friend in the hospital, the cops on my ass and my father dying in an emergency room. Sure, I've come out of this real nice." He took a deep breath and closed his eyes, laying his head back on his hands. "And now Eli knows how to control Morningway. Adams and the others are walking into a trap. Eli's going to double-cross..."

A wave of nausea came over Nathan and he had to hold himself steady on the arm of the couch. "What was that?" As the nausea cleared, he felt a cold chill.

Roland raised an eyebrow. "It's your senses developing," he said. "Getting used to the feel of the city. That'll happen."

"Even buildings and cities have a soul of their own," Libby said.

Nathan sat back and took a few deep breaths. The sensation remained, but became more bearable. "It feels like ... like something's wrong."

Roland nodded. "Yup. Everything you do has a ripple effect, like tossing a rock in a lake. We can pick up on it, the more of your past lives you remember, the easier it gets. You pay attention, focus on the sensations, and you can learn to spot the patterns of a place's energy. When the energy changes, like a building catches fire a few blocks away or that nice old lady across the hall croaks, you can feel it. Some people get so good they can feel the ripples even before something's happened, getting premonitions and such. Most of us learn to accept that we can't always do something about it. This one feels big. Dark magic, ancient hate. People are going to die."

"You mean," Nathan said, "whatever's causing this … ripple is happening right now?"

Roland nodded once and exhaled a large ball of smoke.

"Eli." Nathan's neck twinged. "He's turning on Adams and the others. He's taking control of the soul eater."

"I guess. Could be something else, though. It's hard to say for certain what causes the flow to change, especially in this town. Not unless you're nearby."

"Then it's too late?"

Roland stood to walk over toward the shrine of old mementos. "You never know, kid. Intention's a funny thing. It can shift the mood of a room, ruin a business deal, make a man doubt at the wrong moment. But it takes will to really see you through, to make a difference. Intention *and* the will to use it?" Roland let out a low whistle. "That stuff can change the world."

"You want my advice though," Roland went on, "leave them to it. Adams is a jerk at the best of times, and he shouldn't have brought those people here. New York belongs to the Council. Maybe they'll get lucky and take out Eli or Gideon, bloody Dorian's nose a little, but then they're gone, you know?"

Roland sat back down, across from Nathan, and looked him in the eyes. "You want a piece of good advice, kid? Get out while you've got something left to lose. Go see your old man. If he pulls through, he'll want to see you. If not, well at least you'll get to say goodbye."

For a moment, it was tempting. To think he could leave it alone, leave Adams, Lane, and Cadence to their fate and be with his dad. But then, if his dad didn't make it, what was the point of him having given up his life? What kind of a man would leave good people to die when there was any chance of stopping it?

Not a man raised by Mike Shepherd, that was for sure.

"Some things just have to be done," Nathan said softly, repeating his father's words.

Nathan stepped into Libby's room and examined the sword hanging on the wall. He admired the craftsmanship and the obvious care with which the weapon had been treated over the years.

He reached for the sword and lifted it off the wall. The weight felt good, familiar. He returned to the common room and gave it a couple of swings to feel how it moved. He found it easy to wield, his grip shifting instinctively to support the weapon. He knew this sword.

"This was mine." He saw the sword in a distant memory. Flashes of different lifetimes came to him, settling finally on Katherine O'Reilly. Her training, her compassion and her love infused Nathan.

It all led to this. Every dream, every memory, every bit of research had given him a small taste of this feeling. Katherine O'Reilly wasn't just someone he had been; she was him. Her memories became his, and with them came purpose.

What he was about to do scared the crap out of him.

Most of his past life memories involved him dying horribly in the face of evil. But Morningway had done worse than kill. He had trapped souls, making them suffer indefinitely. That had to stop. And at the moment, Nathan was the only person in the city who had the knowledge needed to stop him, the opportunity to interfere in Eli's plans, and, at last, the will to see it done.

"You're about to go and do something really stupid," Roland said. "Aren't you?"

Nathan looked over at Roland. "I was hoping for a better pep talk than that."

Libby got up and disappeared into her room. She returned with a leather equipment harness that she handed to Nathan.

"You'll need this, too," she said.

She helped him fasten the harness around his torso. It had sheaths and pouches for weapons and tools, along with a sword scabbard clipped on at the waist. Libby gave the straps a few tugs to ensure they were tight and took a step back, nodding in approval.

"There," she said. "That looks like a good fit."

Nathan sheathed the sword in the scabbard and slung his rattan stick bag across his back. He took a deep breath and nodded, standing up straight.

"You could stand to tone up a bit," Libby commented, "maybe lose a little gut. But I wouldn't kick you out of bed. Good luck, Nathan."

"You'll need it," Roland said. "What's your plan?"

"Plan?"

"You're about to go into battle against agents of an ancient organization that controls just about everything in the city. They're fighting for control of a two hundred year old necromancer who turned himself into an unkillable monster that eats souls. Your only allies think you've turned your back on them and are likely to mistake you for another enemy. There'll be guns, swords, magic, and undead soldiers. You don't have the skill or the experience to have a hope of surviving a straight fight. You're outnumbered, outclassed, and you've only begun to reclaim any strength from past lives. Your only chance of pulling this off is a really good plan." Roland lit up another cigarette and took a drag. "So, what is it?"

Nathan thought for a moment.

"I'm going to fuck their shit up," he said.

Roland raised his eyebrows. "Huh. Good plan."

Nathan strode out of the chamber.

Cadence had recovered enough to sit up and help, but her legs refused to work. She and Adams were pinned down behind an excavator. Adams was trading shotgun blasts for pistol shots from Eli and Gideon while the revenants battled the other reborn in close combat. Cadence took shots with her pistol when she could, but she couldn't summon the energy needed to throw in any quick spells that would help the fight. She needed to save her strength for when it would help most.

Lane backed away from Morningway, firing his shotgun. Morningway jerked as the shot struck him, but remained standing. Morningway lunged at Lane and pinned him to the ground. Lane screamed as Morningway's hand reached for his mouth.

Cadence raised her hand and summoned up what power she could. Quick invocations were best kept simple. Elements were the most straightforward to manipulate, and she had a particular talent for using wind and air. Still, it took time to channel enough power for the spell.

Glowing mist flowed from Lane's mouth. His face stretched and twisted in agony, his eyes rolled back in his head. Morningway drew his hand back, taking the glowing mist with it.

Cadence ionized the air, creating a bolt of lightning which arced from the palm of her hand and struck the soul eater. He flew through the air, electricity coursing over and through him. Lane lay still.

"Gods, no." Cadence approached Lane's body. Movement caught her attention. Morningway rose, throwing himself back to his feet. He charged straight toward them.

"Oh, shit," Cadence cried. "Adams, there!"

Adams turned and fired his shotgun, catching Morningway in the face. Morningway fell onto his back and rolled. His shattered face re-formed as he got back to his feet.

Cadence drew up essence from herself for another spell. This time she formed a more stable spell in her mind and blasted Morningway with a stream of electricity from her hands. The soul eater staggered and leaned against the current.

A gunshot rang out. The bullet struck Adams in the side of the head. There was a spray of blood from the exit wound as he fell to the ground.

Cadence felt her pulse race. All around, things were going to hell, fast. Several revenants climbing the crane threw Adams's sniper to his death. Lane wasn't moving. The rest of the reborn weren't exactly shouting out victory cries.

Morningway pressed himself against Cadence's spell and she felt herself straining to keep the flow of energy strong enough to maintain the effect. She saw only two of the reborn still moving. One was helping pull a revenant off another, but was shot in the back by Eli. The revenant lowered its head to the stomach of its victim and she saw the young man try to pull away with one flailing arm. The revenant began to eat him while he was still alive.

Adams's men had taken down about seven of the revenants, from what she could see, but despite their effort they simply hadn't been up to facing off against so many.

Cadence felt the last of her reserves give way. As the spell failed, she prayed that someone would destroy Morningway, freeing her soul to move on.

She felt her senses widen. The cold, heavy energy of the city crushed in around her. But this felt different. A new wind blew in, causing the city's old energy to shift and scatter.

Something was changing.

Someone was coming.

Chapter Seventeen

THE 4X4 HAD BEEN WAITING OUTSIDE FREEDOM Tunnel, the keys in the ignition. It forced Nathan's car off the road, so he had figured it would do to get him quickly into the construction site.

He'd been right.

Nathan drove the car through the barrier, ripping down the wooden panels and powering toward the middle of the site. Stunned faces looked into the light of the car's high-beams and recoiled.

Three men in overalls, their flesh rotten and hanging from their bones, were feasting on the remains of a man. Nathan pressed the accelerator down and smashed through them. One rolled over the hood while another's skull was crushed by the wheels. The third's neck snapped when the car clipped its head.

Cadence lay on the ground right ahead, Morningway nearly on her. His dead face craned around, and he sneered, as though he already knew who was driving the car. Across from them, Eli and Gideon watched from behind the cover of some concrete blocks.

Cadence rolled out of the way. Nathan put the car into top gear and rammed Morningway. The soul eater struck the windshield and cracked the glass, grabbing on to the car before he fell off. He punched a hand through the windscreen, reaching for Nathan, who steered the car toward a line of pre-fabricated office units. If Morningway wanted to play, Nathan was more than willing to oblige.

Nathan opened the car door and jumped. The 4x4 tore into the pre-fabs, tumbling over itself before finally coming to a stop underneath the shattered remains of two of the units.

Rolling to his feet, Nathan broke into a run, back toward Cadence. Two more of the revenants ran at him. He drew his rattan sticks without stopping. He was ready for the first one and whipped a rattan stick across its face. Something cracked. The revenant fell to one side. The second was a little faster and ducked when Nathan swung at it.

Beyond the revenant, Nathan saw Gideon lining up a shot with his pistol, then heard several gunshots. Gideon jerked as bullets hit him. Cadence was holding herself up against an excavator, firing at Gideon, who spun and fired twice in her direction. One of the rounds caught her high in the chest and she fell back onto the ground.

Nathan dropped one of his rattan sticks and drew his sword. He slashed open the revenant's neck with the draw. Its head fell back while it staggered away. Nathan pushed himself on, adrenaline coursing through him, giving him a speed and agility he'd never known he possessed.

He jumped onto a waist-high stack of wooden pallets and leaped at Gideon, landing on the vampire with a solid kick to the chest. Both men tumbled to the ground and Nathan pressed a rattan stick against Gideon's throat. Eli backed away, smirking as he tossed aside his spent pistol. Gideon flashed a snarl in Eli's direction and then brought his knee up between Nathan's legs.

Nathan fell and curled into a fetal position. Gideon snatched the rattan stick and snapped it in two, dropping the pieces.

"Cocky bastard," Gideon growled. He kicked Nathan twice in the stomach but when he tried for a third, Nathan caught his leg and twisted, pulling the vampire off balance and bringing him to the ground.

Without hesitating, Nathan picked up one of the broken rattan pieces and drove the piece into his chest. Gideon screamed in pain and convulsed, roaring obscenities in several languages.

He didn't die right away, not like the vampire Nathan's father had staked. Instead, he fell silent and still. He appeared dead, but Nathan didn't want to take any chances and retrieved his sword to hack Gideon's head from his body. It took two swings, but once the head was removed, the body began to quickly decay and turn to dust and smoke. Nathan turned to face Eli.

"You think you're something special, don't you?" Eli grinned. "Think you're the first to try and be the hero, to try to kill me?" He drew his sword, a long saber.

"No," Nathan said. "But I'll be the last."

He raised his sword and waited, out of fear as much as anything. Up to now, he'd been running on adrenaline and the element of surprise. He'd fought his way past the revenants and killed Gideon with blind fury and chance. This would be different. Eli was ready, in a position to defend himself and fight back.

"And who exactly are you to think you can take me?" Eli's eyes shifted to blood red. "On your knees, mortal. You are *my* prey."

Nathan didn't move. "Sorry. Some friends cleaned up that nasty bite you gave me. I am nobody's prey."

"You think you knew me once," Eli said. "Don't you?"

"Once you called me Silver."

"Ah yes. As I recall, I killed him."

"I figured it was time for round two."

Eli snarled and ran at him, sweeping his saber down and to the right. He deflected the blow and attempted to counter, but Eli was fast and skilled. He moved his sword with incredible precision, parrying Nathan's strikes and meting out light blows of his own as though testing Nathan's skill. Eli cut Nathan's leg just below the knee. The pain caused him to drop his guard.

Eli punched Nathan in the face, using the hand-guard of his sword as a crude bludgeon. The metal cut into his left cheekbone and he stumbled. Eli pressed his attack, slashing Nathan's ribs. He chopped downward. Nathan held his sword up so the blow struck only steel. Eli kicked the wound he'd just given Nathan on his ribs and then swatted the sword from Nathan's grip, cutting the back of Nathan's right hand as he did.

The pain made it difficult to move. Nathan reached for his sword, but Eli kicked him in the jaw, bloodying his mouth. He felt cold steel against his throat and looked up. Eli looked at ease, while Nathan was bleeding and in too much pain to take a full breath.

Nathan had been going without sleep. He'd fought harder than in even the longest sparring sessions back at the dojo, and now he had a sword held to his neck. The spot where Eli's bite had been burned away ached.

Eli flicked his eyes toward the crashed SUV. "Morningway," he called. "I command you to kill Cadence Brooke."

The remains of the prefabs shook and Morningway climbed out from the rubble. He walked down from the wreckage toward Cadence, who lay helpless, one hand pressed firmly against the bullet wound below her collarbone. She looked pale and afraid.

"Please help, Nathan. Please..."

How many of Nathan's lives had ended like this? Lying at the foot of an enemy, utterly beaten.

"First her," Eli said. "Then you. Then anyone who gets in the Council's way."

Nathan thought back to his lives as Lucius and Katherine. Both times he had been killed by an enemy far stronger than him. Both times he had sacrificed his life for nothing.

No. Not for nothing.

More images surged through Nathan's mind. Thoughts and memories of other battles, other challenges, times when defeat was not the end. As Katherine O'Reilly he had saved lives, trained and taught people to protect themselves. As Lucius, he had led men into victorious battle against brutal warlords.

Nathan found himself kneeling in the snow. Avitus walked away, having just delivered a blow they both knew was mortal. This time, however, Nathan remembered how he had looked up, and he saw past his enemy.

Avitus turned toward huddled women, who held out their arms in a vain attempt to protect their young children. The women were tired, cold, and hungry but defiant all the same. The things Avitus would do to them, and have many of his men do, would be unforgivable.

So Lucius, a dying man, did the only thing he knew how.

He stood up, and lifted his sword.

With the last measure of strength he had left, Lucius gave a wordless cry and charged. Avitus turned and everything slowed down. Lucius struck with unbearable fury, swinging his sword with such ferocity that Avitus was beaten back. Lucius split one of his knees, then hacked his wrist, before thrusting his sword between the joints in his foe's amour, stabbing him in the belly.

Avitus fell, and Lucius stood.

Lucius walked to the women and knelt, leaning on his sword. "I shed my blood for you," he said. "For those oppressed by tyrants, for those abused by the strong. I ask you to remember this." He looked up at a woman, beautiful despite the dirt and tears on her face. "Remember."

Lucius and Avitus died next to one another.

Remember.

A new feeling came over Nathan. The memory became a part of him. He reached back into those memories, the deeds and strengths of past lives, and found a new power.

His muscles no longer ached. His vision no longer blurred. His pain no longer mattered. Nathan took into himself those things that had made those people great. He felt the change and knew they were with him now. He had Lucius's strength and Katherine's speed. He saw their greatest victories through their eyes as he took up his sword once more and faced Eli. Nathan's eyes were cold with resolution and renewed strength. Eli's resolve faltered before Nathan's glare, his eyes starting to tremble. Nathan saw recognition in his face.

"No," Eli stammered. "I don't believe it."

"Yes, you do," Nathan's voice resonated with power. "That's why you're afraid."

Nathan stood tall and renewed his attack. With one stroke of his sword, he knocked Eli's weapon to one side, then ducked under the counter-attack to slash his hamstring. His legs buckled, and Nathan took his sword in an overhead swing, cutting deep into the flesh between the vampire's neck and shoulder. Stepping around Eli, Nathan completed a full circle and cut downward. Eli cried out in pain and held up his ruined hand, now cut in half.

Nathan drew his sword back. "This is for my father."

The cut was clean and quick, but still satisfying. Nathan took Eli's head in one stroke, leaving his remains to fall into dust and scatter in the wind.

Morningway stopped, just as he was stooping over Cadence. He looked back at Nathan and cocked his head.

Nathan saw a familiar pendant, shaped like a dragonfly, in the dust that had been Eli. He picked it up in his left hand, still holding the sword in his right.

The soul eater approached Nathan, reaching out with grasping hands. "Give that to me," Morningway rasped.

"Sorry, Tad," he said, "We left something unfinished once before. It's time to put things right."

Nathan dropped the pendant onto a stack of wooden pallets and crushed it with a lump of masonry. There was a brilliant flash of light that threatened to blind him. The blue burst tore into Morningway with a baleful howl as his ancient flesh was ripped from his bones, which shattered into thousands of pieces and were lost in a swirling vortex of wind and light.

When the wind settled, illuminated figures surrounded Nathan in the glowing light. He knew who they were.

Three approached, their hands held up as if to reach for him. The first was a woman - Miranda Grange.

She wore a light summer dress, not the combat fatigues or arsenal Nathan would have expected. Next to her, the form of Jim Lane reached for her hand. Their fingers intertwined and they closed their eyes.

Glowing, semi-transparent figures gathered around Nathan and stood in silence, their faces beaming with joy and relief. The normally heavy and oppressive weight of New York's energy was, for now at least, pushed aside by feelings of gratitude.

Another person walked forward, her hands clasped together under her chin. Nathan knew her too. Elisabeth Morningway. She mouthed the words "thank you," and bowed her head. She'd been Morningway's prisoner for a hundred and fifty years.

One by one, the shimmering ghosts turned and faded away. There was no pillar of light, no opening in the heavens or shining portal leading them to whatever lay beyond this world. They simply vanished.

Lane and Miranda were the last to leave. Miranda blew a kiss to Nathan and waved. Lane tipped his forehead in salute, and they were gone.

Three battered revenants approached cautiously. Nathan lifted his sword and pointed it at them. "You want to try it?"

The revenants were smarter than they looked, or dumber, and fell for his bluff. Nathan was exhausted and the pain of his injuries was returning with a vengeance. He felt in no state to fight, but the revenants were intimidated and stopped, hissing at Nathan.

"You go back to Dorian," he said. "Tell him he lost."

The revenants crept away, leaving Nathan alone with Cadence. She was alive but had lost a lot of blood.

"What was that?" she asked.

"I'm not really sure," Nathan said. "But we need to get that wound looked at."

"Can't go to a regular hospital."

"It's okay, I know a guy who's really good." He helped Cadence up. By the time they'd gotten into Adams's rented car and driven away, police sirens wailed in the distance.

Chapter Eighteen

Michael Joseph Shepherd was laid to rest four days later.

He was buried in a small family plot next to his wife, Louise. It was a sunny day, and there was a huge turnout. Nathan had never thought about how many lives his father had touched, how many people respected him or owed their lives to him. He received full honors from his old firefighter unit.

Of Nathan's friends, only Cynthia turned up. He hadn't been expecting to see her, considering her injuries, but he was glad she came. She had to use a wheelchair because her leg was still in a cast. Most of the small cuts on her face hadn't needed stitches and would heal well. Her left arm hung in a sling tied around her neck, while her right hand and forearm were wrapped in tight bandages. She looked pale and tired, which she insisted was a result of her pain medication.

After the funeral, Nathan spoke to the people who'd come to see his father off. Old friends from his unit were there, of course, and Nathan met the man who Mike had asked to be the manager for his bar. A number of people from Mike's neighborhood attended. They were an eclectic bunch; some of them looked more like they were dressed for a court appearance for petty theft instead of a funeral, but they seemed like good people. Nathan learned that a lot of them had been, or knew someone who had been, saved by Mike in the fire that had forced him into early retirement. They expressed their gratitude and admiration for Nathan's father before leaving quietly.

The police had questioned Nathan about the string of unexplained deaths, but the case was dropped. Detective Powell had been pretty pissed off. Nathan suspected Dorian's influence was to thank for it. He felt sick at the idea of owing Dorian anything, but it made sense that he'd want the police staying out of his business.

With all the questioning in the murder investigation, Nathan had missed more work. His boss finally lost his patience and fired him. He'd seen it coming, and hoped the inheritance his father had left him would see him through until he could find another job.

Cadence was fine. The bullet didn't hit anything vital. It was the week after the funeral when Nathan brought her to Grand Central Station to get the train back to Boston. Her right arm was bound to her torso so she wouldn't pull at the sutures and Nathan had insisted that she spend some time resting before going home.

"You could come with me," Cadence said as they walked to the platform. "We could use you. And it'd be nice if someone had my back when I try to explain things to the Boston Conclave."

"I don't think I'd fit in. Besides, this is home, you know? And I've got to stick around at least until everything's settled with Laura."

"I'm so sorry."

"The fact we're not married makes some things easier and some things more complicated. She wants the house, and she's offered to pay me for it. I could use the cash now."

"If you need anything just call. You've done a great thing, for all of us."

She gave Nathan a one-armed hug and a kiss on the cheek before boarding her train. He waved goodbye and left, turning to find Roland watching.

"What happens now?" Roland asked.

"Damned if I know," Nathan said. "This sort of thing happen a lot?"

"What, people show up, kill a monster, then leave? Sure. Not in New York for a while, but we're kinda short on people who give a damn about this kind of thing."

"You think you've got problems. I've got no job, my girlfriend is having my best friend's baby, and the best sex I've had was a hundred and eighty years ago. When I was a woman."

Roland laughed as they headed to the exit. "Shit happens, kid. Things will settle down in a while. Dorian's claiming Eli acted on his own, that his instructions had been to help Adams destroy the soul eater, not to try and control it. The official story is that he's grateful to the reborn for their help, sorry for their losses, yadda yadda, he'll make some kind of compensation."

"Probably why he got the cops off my back," Nathan said. "If that's the official story, what about unofficially?"

Roland ignored a No Smoking sign and lit up as they passed through the terminal. "The way you tell it, Dorian was head over heels in love with Elisabeth Morningway, who loved him back, even though she was married to Thaddeus. He took her as his first kill, and her soul was bound to his phylactery ever since. You freed her, which means, as far as Dorian's concerned, that you tossed the soul of the woman he loved into oblivion, never to be found again."

"Sounds about fair to me," Nathan said, remembering Dorian's betrayal of Katherine and Malcolm.

"Dorian won't see it like that. He'll have to leave you alone for now, because the Council is pretty glad Morningway's dead, but he'll jump at the chance to take you down if it presents itself. He might even try and trick you into making a move against the Council and bringing their wrath down on yourself."

Nathan sighed. "Fantastic."

"But you should be okay," Roland continued. "If you stick to your plan. Live a nice mundane life, forget about Dorian, and let things get back to normal around here."

Nathan could walk away. It wasn't like things were going to get worse in New York. After all, the bad guy was dead, and the Council was down a couple of vampires. With Cadence on her way back to Boston, The Lost could stay as they'd been for the last decade or so, along with every other everyday person living with a society of immortal supernatural predators looking down on them, using them as food or for their own entertainment. Life would go on, with the weak suffering under the heels of the strong, like they had done throughout history.

Could Nathan walk away from that?

No.

Dorian looked out at his city. Its lights gleamed below, held aloft on towers of glass and steel. To the mundane eye nothing had changed. To senses honed over centuries of training in the dark arts, the city was being swept up in a storm of chaos and disruption. All because of one damned office clerk who had to get in the way.

Creek had been waiting patiently while Dorian sipped whiskey. He coughed once and Dorian turned.

"Has everything been done?" Dorian asked him.

"Yes, my Lord. But there is still the matter of Shepherd. The High Council has denied your request to pursue him."

"Not the right political move." Dorian eased into a luxurious leather chair. "We'll watch him for now. He's been through a lot, and he's alone. I'd be surprised if he doesn't drink himself to death in a week."

"And if he surprises us again, sir?" said Creek.

"Then we draw him in." Dorian inhaled deeply, closing his eyes. "We'll take him, break him, and maybe when I've grown bored of him, I'll let him die."

"And your prize?"

"Lost. Forever."

"Understood." Creek placed a manila folder on Dorian's desk. "This is what we have on the current state of affairs. I'll be in my office for the next hour if you need anything."

Dorian dismissed Creek with a wave of his hand and sat alone in darkness for some time. A soft glow appeared before him on the other side of the window. Slowly it resolved into the form of a beautiful young woman in a mid 19th-century dress. Dorian stood and walked to the window. With shaking hands, he touched his fingers against the glass. "Elisabeth."

She mirrored his movements, sadness marring her features.

"I tried. I tried to save you."

She nodded.

"I love you." Dorian withdrew his hand and clenched his fist. "I always will."

Elisabeth held up her hand as she faded from sight.

"Lost. Forever."

Candles and braziers lit the chamber deep inside Freedom Tunnel. Nathan turned to look at Roland, who watched from a corner. Kian and Danielle stood on either side of Nathan while Libby walked a circle around him, looking him up and down. He was dressed in dark, functional clothing. She nodded and motioned to Kian, who handed him the leather utility harness he'd worn before.

He strapped on the harness, fastening it tightly. It was filled with a collection of tools and useful items, as well as a knife tucked into a sheath at the small of his back.

Libby nodded to Danielle, who handed Nathan a folded up bundle. He took it and held it up. It was his father's old hooded duffel coat, though there had been some modifications to lengthen it and pad the lining with protective armor. He put the coat on, finding that it still smelled of his father. The extra padding made the coat heavier, but he could still move easily.

Finally, Libby held up Nathan's sword and presented it to him. He took it and slid it into its sheath on the harness, then closed it over his coat.

There were no words spoken. Nathan looked up at the collection of mementos from others who had died trying to change things in the city and made his silent oath. He turned and walked back to the main tunnel, passing the people huddled around fires, all watching as he went by. With each step he grew more and more resilient, determined to keep going. As he passed the rest of The Lost, Nathan felt the shift in their feelings, knowing that they understood his intent and that they accepted him. Fear and mistrust left their faces, a sliver of hope shining in their eyes as they watched him leave and walk out into the night.

They were his to protect, now, along with all of the people he passed on the streets. Nathan knew that his presence would not go unnoticed, not now. Not ever. He had nothing left. Nothing but the city streets. He would be a shadow to the bright lights of the Council's towers.

Wherever they crossed the line and allowed an innocent to suffer, he would be there, moving between the forgotten places and lost alleyways.

He was Lucius Appianus. He was Daniel Silver. He was Katherine O'Reilly. He was all of these people and more. Their strength was his. Their knowledge would guide him. Their power would become his own, unlocked for him to wield, to protect those who could not protect themselves, until the day he died.

And every lifetime ever after.

Acknowledgements

THIS BOOK IS THE END RESULT OF YEARS OF DEDICATION and dreams. However, as much work as I put into it there simply wouldn't be a book if not for the support and advice of others.

I'd like to thank Ellen Brickley and Aislinn O'Loughlin Scanlon for happily listening to me ramble on and on about my ideas and helping me put those ideas together on the page. My beta readers, David O'Brien, Aonghus Collins, Maria Mello Rella, Patricia McMullin and Janto McMullin. You gave me the objective viewpoints I needed. Karen Jones Gowen, for hosting the contest which resulted in my book deal. Allie Maldonado for having faith in the manuscript. Bruce Gowen for his marketing advice, and of course my amazing editors, Kristine Princevalle and Amie McCracken.

I have to also thank my sister, Tanya, and my parents, Tony and Georgina. Thank you for letting me dream.

And of course, my wife, Jen. You've been my strongest supporter as long as we've been together. I couldn't imagine anyone else I'd want by my side on this journey. You make every good thing better.

And thank you to all my friends and family who've been there for me over the last couple of years. It's been harder than I've let on at times, but I love you all and I wouldn't be here without you.

Lightning Source UK Ltd.
Milton Keynes UK
UKOW040403261012

201227UK00001B/15/P